A BUNCH OF FUN DRAMAS

Wanda Pearce

BROADMAN PRESS
Nashville, Tennessee

© Copyright 1990 ● Broadman Press
All rights reserved
4275-28
ISBN: 0-8054-7528-1
Dewey Decimal Classification: 812
Subject Heading: DRAMA — COLLECTED WORKS
Library of Congress Catalog Card Number: 89-33094
Printed in the United States of America

Library of Congress Cataloging-in-Publication Data
Pearce, Wanda, 1928-
    A bunch of fun dramas / Wanda Pearce.
        p.   cm.
   ISBN 0-8054-7528-1
    1. Christian drama, American. 2. Young adult drama,
American.
    3. Drama in Christian education. 4. Improvisation (Acting)
I. Title.
PS3566.E217B86   1990 89-33094
812'.54—dc20 . . . . CIP

To my husband Ray, who encourages me
constantly with his love and laughter . . .

. . . to my sons, their wives, and their children
who truly have the gift of laughter . . .

. . . and to Mary Cate Abington
and Carolyn Brakeville Taylor
with whom I shared many hours of hilarity
as we prepared for
banquets and choir parties, etc., at First Baptist Church
in DeQueen, Arkansas.

Preface

Dear Readers:

It is my deepest wish that you find enjoyment from the material in this book. Most of it was written for a specific occasion. I encourage you to write your own material, or at least combine and use material you can find and make it your own.

Most of all, I hope you will see Christian lives enriched by "playing" together. It is a necessity of the spirit at any age. It helps break down walls and deepens friendship even in those who are "just watching." It becomes a shared, joyful experience.

Please share these times with people who do not know God's love in a personal way. Show them the laughter and good times Christians have together. This is one of the beautiful gifts God has given us.

Thank you for letting me share these good times with you.

WANDA PEARCE

CONTENTS

I. EVENING-LENGTH FUN DRAMAS

II. FUN DRAMAS SHORTER IN LENGTH

III. IMPROMPTU DRAMA WITH A NARRATOR

IV. RAPS

V. IDEAS FOR SHARING

I.

EVENING-LENGTH FUN DRAMAS

Moonlight and Magnolia

(The story that asks the question: "Did Rhitt really die or just fade away?")

CHARACTERS

MAGNOLIA WRIGHT: *young and beautiful, apparently a widow*
RACHEL: *Magnolia's cousin*
PRISSY: *Magnolia's faithful maid*
PERCY: *cousin to Magnolia, wealthy and selfish*
AUNT CAROLINE: *Percy's mother, wealthy and selfish*
THADDEUS THACKERY: *the town's leading lawyer, greedy and selfish*
RHITT WRIGHT: *Magnolia's lost husband*
NARRATOR

SETTING

Veranda of the old plantation

PROPS

Chairs on a porch for Scenes 1 and 4. A coffee service and chairs indoors for Scene 2. Chairs and a desk or a small table for Scene 3.

SCENE 1

On the veranda

NARRATOR: Continuing the gripping saga of life in a typical

Southern town, on a typical southern plantation, with typical characters, after the typical Civil War. Very typical! Listen as Rachel says . . .

RACHEL: Oh, Magnolia, how will we keep from starving? No one to plant the cotton. Rhitt has died. Oh, poor little me! Oh, whatever shall we do?

MAGNOLIA: Now, Rachel . . . I'll find a way.

PRISSY: My, my, Miss Magnolia . . . they just ain't nothin' to eat!

MAGNOLIA: Wait, Prissy. Look! Who is that comin' yonder?

RACHEL: Why, it looks like . . .

PRISSY: Mercy me! It look like . . .

MAGNOLIA: It's Rhitt! He's alive! He's come home . . . we're saved!

(*Magnolia rushes to embrace Rhitt. He stands with hands to his sides as if dazed. He looks blank and mutters questions like "Who am I?" "Where am I?" "Who are you?" "What's my name?"*)

MAGNOLIA: Why, Rhitt, don't you know me? I'm Magnolia, your young and beautiful wife!

RACHEL: Magnolia . . . he . . . has amnesia.

PRISSY: My, my, Miss Magnolia. What'll we do? Mr. Rhitt has am . . . nes . . . ia. Is it catchin'? And there ain't nothin' to eat. Oh, what'll we do? (*Blackout*)

(*Music to bridge scenes*)

SCENE 2

The cousins' mansion

PERCY: Welcome to our mansion, Cousin Magnolia. I'm sorry to hear about Rhitt. It's just tragic. But that's life.

AUNT CAROLINE: Dear Magnolia. You have really suffered. Rhitt gone so long. And then, when he did return—amnesia! But that's life.

MAGNOLIA: (*Sarcastically*) Yes, dear Auntie and Cousin Percy. We all have our burdens to bear. But with generous relatives such as you, life becomes a little easier.

PERCY: Generous? Uh . . . ah . . . well . . . Cousin Magnolia, we had a bad year last year. The cotton crop just didn't come up to expectations . . . you know.

AUNT CAROLINE: But if you need any old clothes or anything, we can manage.

MAGNOLIA: Everything would be just fine if I only knew where Rhitt buried all our money before the Yankees came. Why, there must be thousands! Maybe he'll get his memory back, and we'll know soon.

PERCY: Why, Cousin Magnolia! Money buried on your property?

MAGNOLIA: Yes, Rhitt buried thousands!

PERCY: You don't know where?

MAGNOLIA: Somewhere—probably put it in the fields.

AUNT CAROLINE: Uh, Percy, don't you think you might spare a few men for *plowing* and planting the cotton for dear Magnolia? After all, we are family!

(*Magnolia turns to audience and smiles slyly.*)

(*Blackout*)

(*Music*)

SCENE 3

NARRATOR: The scene is the office of Thaddeus Thackery: lawyer, ladies' man, and sleaze bucket.

MAGNOLIA: Thaddeus, I just had to come to you and tell you about Rhitt. You've been so sympathetic all the time he was missing. You are a good friend, Thaddeus.

THADDEUS: My sweet Magnolia. It was my pleasure! Too bad about Rhitt's memory.

MAGNOLIA: Yes, we have no money and no way to plant the cotton crop. But with good, generous friends like you, I'm sure there must be a way.

THADDEUS: Well, Magnolia, I haven't been able to collect any fees lately. Expenses are terrible. And you know the Yankees nearly wiped me out!

MAGNOLIA: Oh, Thaddeus, everything would be all right if only Rhitt would regain his memory, so he could tell us where he buried the money.

THADDEUS: The money? What money?

MAGNOLIA: Oh, just thousands and thousands!

THADDEUS: Magnolia, my sweet, don't you know where he buried it?

MAGNOLIA: No. Thaddeus. He didn't tell me, and now he can't remember. But it must have been out in some of the cotton fields.

THADDEUS: Uh . . . Magnolia, I think maybe I could spare a few men to help you plow and plant your cotton fields. In fact, I might come out there and help oversee the situation.

MAGNOLIA: Oh, Thaddeus! You are so generous!

(*Again Magnolia turns to audience and smiles slyly.*)

(*Blackout*)

(*Music*)

SCENE 4

On the veranda

NARRATOR: Lovely, sweet Magnolia. We find her, Rachel, and Prissy on the veranda of the plantation. It is some weeks later. Rhitt is wandering around aimlessly. (*Rhitt keeps repeating former monologue.*)

RACHEL: Magnolia, isn't it wonderful that Cousin Percy and Mr. Thackery came to our rescue? Why, they have been out in the fields working and working for days.

PRISSY: My, my, it's good to have somethin' to eat.

MAGNOLIA: Yes, they are generous gentlemen. Here they come now.

(*Enter Percy and Thaddeus T. They look tired and disheveled, but determined.*)

PERCY: Magnolia, the cotton is just about planted on the north forty, and we haven't found . . . I mean we'll be through soon. Are you sure Rhitt doesn't remember where he buried the money?

MAGNOLIA: I'll call him. He's around here some place.

(*She calls him. He continues: "Who am I?" etc.*)

THADDEUS: Oh, he's an idiot. We'll never get anything out of him!

(*All actors freeze.*)

(*Blackout*)

(*Music*)

SCENE V

SETTING: same as Scene IV

NARRATOR: Time passes, the fall harvesting is finished, and the cotton crop is good. Magnolia has saved the plantation and amassed a great fortune.

(*Percy and Thaddeus look even more disheveled. Magnolia and the other women are dancing around a basket of money. Rhitt has amazingly recovered.*)

MAGNOLIA: Oh, Rhitt, my darling, all is well. The plantation is saved, you've recovered your memory, and we have such generous friends. Isn't life wonderful!

RHITT: Yes, I want to thank you, Cousin Percy and Thaddeus, for taking such good care of the plantation and Magnolia while I was away and ill.

(*Percy and Thaddeus mutter under their breath and slink away.*)

PRISSY: My, my, Miss Magnolia. Let's eat!

NARRATOR: They lived happily ever after, and no one knew where Rhitt hid his money. But Magnolia knew how to find it!

For Whom the Bell Tolls or Will Nellie Swing Tonight?

CHARACTERS

LITTLE NELL
DUDLEY DO-RIGHT
DASTARDLY DAN
FARMER JOHN
MRS. FARMER JOHN
CONSTABLE

SETTING

The front porch of farmhouse

PROPS

Two chairs (*rocking chairs if possible*), door at back of set.

SCENE 1

MRS. FARMER JOHN: Oh, Pa, whut air we gonna do? The cow's gone dry, the chickens won't lay, and we done et the last of the pork 'n beans.

FARMER JOHN: I tell ya, Ma, ya jes cain't depend on nuthin' (*sigh*). Whar's Nellie, Ma?

MRS. FARMER JOHN: You mean our bee-you-tiful, sweet, shy daughter who looks and acts jes like her ma?

FARMER JOHN: Yes, dear Nellie! She's our only hope! If she kin marry a rich, fine upstandin' boy with lots of money, we'll be saved.

MRS. FARMER JOHN: Hyar comes Nellie now, but she's with that Dudley—pore but proud—Do-Right. Now if she'd jes marry Dastardly Dan we'd be set fer life.

FARMER JOHN: Now, Ma, ya know I don't trust Dastardly Dan. He's been tryin' to buy the mortgage on this hyar farm. He's up to no good!

Enter Nell and Dudley)

NELL: Oh, Dudley, I'm so glad you came over.

DUDLEY: Don't I come ever Tuesday?

NELL: Yes. (*Shyly*) You kin help me with the milkin'.

DUDLEY: Yeah!

NELL: Oh, Dudley, it's springtime! Don't you feel different?

DUDLEY: Uh-huh. My red flannels is itchin'!

NELL: Oh, Dudley, this evenin' was just made for romance!

DUDLEY: Uh . . . ah, Nellie . . .

NELL: (*Tenderly*) Yes, Dudley?

DUDLEY: Uh . . . I wanted to ask you for a long time . . .

NELL: Yes, Dudley, whut?

DUDLEY: Uh . . . some night soon . . . uh . . . I was wonderin'. . . uh . . . if . . .

NELL: Yes, Dudley, whut?

DUDLEY: Uh . . . I was wonderin' if . . . uh. . . if I could hold your hand!

NELL: Why, Dudley, Darlin'! I knowed you hadn't been comin' over hyar fourteen years without something on your mind!

DUDLEY: Mercy! Let's go do the milkin'!

MRS. FARMER JOHN: Wait, Dudley! Didn't you know the cow's gone dry, and the chickens won't lay, and we done et the last of the pork 'n beans?

DUDLEY: Well, ya jest cain't depend on nuthin'!

FARMER JOHN: Dudley, Son! You been sparkin' our Nell for fourteen years now. Whut air yore intentions?

DUDLEY: Intentions? Why, I got good intentions, Sir! I'd do anything in the world for this gal! I'd climb the highest mountain, I'd swim the deepest ocean, I'd go through far (fire) and storm for Li'l Nell!

FARMER JOHN: Wal, Dudley, that's fine, but air ya gonna marry her?

DUDLEY: Wal, now . . . uh . . . ah . . .

NELL: Oh, Dudley, air ya triflin' with my affections?

DUDLEY: Triflin'? Why, Nell! How can ya say such a thing? Why, I'd climb the highest mountain, swim the deepest ocean . . .

NELL (*interrupting*): Oh, Dudley, but will ya marry me?

DUDLEY: Wal . . . uh . . . ah . . . ahem

(*Enter Dastardly Dan*)

DASTARDLY DAN: Oh-ho, me proud beauty! At last I have ya in me power? Marry me or else!

NELL: Or else whut?

DASTARDLY DAN: I have the mortgage on yore farm, and if ya don't marry me, I'll evict ya!

NELL: No! No! A thousand times no!

DASTARDLY DAN: Yes! Yes!

NELL: No! No!

(*Several interchanges of yes-yes and no-no*)

DUDLEY: Well, Nellie, I see yore busy, I'd better be goin'! I'll see ya next Tuesday. (*Blackout*)

SCENE 2

DASTARDLY DAN: Farmer John, give me Nellie, and I'll tear up the mortgage!

FARMER JOHN: No! No! You're an evil (emphasis on *vil*) man, Dastardly Dan!

DASTARDLY DAN: Whut do ya say, Mrs. Farmer John?

MRS. FARMER JOHN: Oh, Dastardly, the cow's gone dry, the chickens won't lay, and we've done et the last of the pork 'n beans!

DASTARDLY DAN: Yep, I know, Mrs. Farmer John. But I'll take care of ya. Here ya are. (*Hands* MRS. JOHN *a can of pork and beans.*)

MRS. FARMER JOHN: Oh, Dastardly! Yore all heart!

FARMER JOHN: Now, Ma, don't be taken in by pretty gifts! He's up to no good!

NELL: Oh, Pa, do I hafta marry Dastardly?

FARMER JOHN: No! No! a thousand times no!

MRS. FARMER JOHN: Yes! Yes!

(*Again interchanges between yes and no*)

DASTARDLY DAN: Now, me proud beauty, I got ya in my power!

(*He drags* NELL *offstage.* FARMER JOHN *follows. Sound of train, screaming.* FARMER JOHN *enters, with* NELL *holding him up.*)

MRS. FARMER JOHN: Oh, Pa, whut happened?

FARMER JOHN: Ma, ya know thet track in our backyard? Wal, they put a train on it, and (*sob*) I pushed Dastardly on the track—and the train run over him—pore Dastardly!

(*Enter* CONSTABLE, *bustling importantly*)

CONSTABLE: Wal, I guess ya know whut this means, Farmer John. Ya killed kindly old Dastardly Dan, so ya'll have to go with me.

FARMER JOHN: No! No! Constable, this don't mean . . .

CONSTABLE (*Regretfully*): Yes . . .

NELL: No! No!

CONSTABLE: Yes!

MRS. FARMER JOHN: But whut'll happen to me?

CONSTABLE (*Ignoring* MRS. JOHN): When the curfew bell rings tonight, you must die for doin' in Dastardly Dan!

MRS. FARMER JOHN: But whut'll happen to me?

NELL: If only Dudley was hyar!

(*Offstage, clomping is heard.*)

NELL: Thar's Dudley now! Oh, Dudley, do somethin'!

(*She falls into his arms.*)

DUDLEY: Now, Dudley, they jest ain't nuthin' ya kin do! He's guilty, and he's gotta hang when th' curfew bell rings tonight!

(CONSTABLE *and* FARMER JOHN *slowly walk offstage.* NELL *and* MRS. JOHN *cry,* DUDLEY *thinks.*)

NELL (*Brightening*): I got a idea.

DUDLEY: Yeah, I got a idea, too.

MRS. FARMER JOHN: Wal, that's somethin' different! Tain't easy for either of ya!

DUDLEY: I gotta go now. Don't you fret, gal! I'll save yer paw! Ya know I'd do anythang in the world fer ya. I'd climb the highest mountain, swim the deepest ocean . . . .

NELL: Oh, Dudley, not now!

(DUDLEY *leaves.* NELL *turns to* MRS. JOHN.)

NELL: The curfew bell will never ring tonight!

(*Blackout*)

SCENE 3

(Scene is same setting. MRS. FARMER JOHN and CONSTABLE are on porch)

CONSTABLE: Wal, it won't be long now, ma'am. It's 5:45, and th' curfew bell rings at 6:00.

MRS. FARMER JOHN (*Looking up*): Constable, who is that climbin' up the bell tower?

CONSTABLE: Up the bell tower? Why, Ma'am, thet's . . . thet's Nellie, ain't it?

MRS. FARMER JOHN: My li'l Nell. She's gone crazy! Come down, Nell, oh, come down!

NELL (*Offstage from a distance as echo*): The curfew bell will never ring tonight!

CONSTABLE: Why, she's tying herself to the clapper of the bell, so it won't ring, and her pa won't hang!

MRS. FARMER JOHN: Oh, thet's jes like Nell, always hangin' around, waitin' for a ring!

(DUDLEY *rushes in. He is dragging* DASTARDLY DAN *with him.*)

DUDLEY: Wait! Wait! Let Farmer John go! Constable, Dastardly only pretended to die, so he'd get the farm and Nell!

MRS. FARMER JOHN: Whut a dastardly thing to do, Dastardly!

DASTARDLY DAN: Curses! Foiled again! Gimme back my pork 'n beans!

CONSTABLE: Yore gonna need 'em! Let's go! (*He and* DASTARDLY DAN *leave.*)

MRS. FARMER JOHN and DUDLEY (*Calling to* NELL): Nellie! Nellie! Ya kin come down now! Yore paw is saved.

(NELL *staggers in.*)

NELL: Oh, Dudley! My hero! (NELL *and* DUDLEY *embrace.*)

(FARMER JOHN *enters, and he and* MRS. FARMER JOHN *embrace.*)

FARMER JOHN: Thank ya, Chillun! Ya saved my life! But tell me, how did ya know where to find Dastardly Dan?

DUDLEY: Wal, ya know I'd do anythang' in the world for this gal. I'd climb the highest mountain, swim the deepest ocean . . . so I jes climbed the mountain, and thar he wuz!

EVERETT ROBERTSON is the author of this fun drama which first appeared in his book, *Extra Dimensions in Church Drama* (Nashville: Convention Press, 1977) pp. 80-81. © Copyright 1977 ● The Baptist Sunday School Board of the Southern Baptist Convention. All rights reserved. Used by permission.

Gunsmoke on the Proponderosa

A playlet depicting how it might have been—but probably was not quite—"out West" a hundred years ago

CHARACTERS

Scene 1:
BAN CARTWHEEL
MOSS CARTWHEEL
LITTLE MOE CARTWHEEL
HIP SANG, their cook
SHERIFF ROY TOFFEE

Scene 2:
LONE STRANGER
PRONTO: larger than the Lone Stranger, with a big broken feather in his headband

Scene 3:
MARSHAL FATT KILLON
CHASTER
MISS KATTY

Scene 4:
WAITER
TELEGRAPH CLERK
CLARKE GOODEPANTS (GOODY)
DEADEYE DICK
LORETTA LOUISE

CLARKE'S HORSE

Scene 5:
MISS SARAH BETH: *schoolmarm*
All other characters

PROPS

sack
tomahawk
gun

SCENE 1

(BAN and MOSS CARTWHEEL are on stage, sitting at a table, eating.)

BAN: Moss, after we get the barn roof patched up tomorrow, we better start moving that herd out of the north pasture. The army will pay well for that beef.

MOSS (*never stopping his eating*): Yeah, Paw, we sure have had good luck with that herd.

(*Sound of horse running offstage.* LITTLE MOE *runs in through the door.*)

MOE: Paw, somebody's stolen half the herd in the north pasture!

BAN (*rising quickly*): What? Moe, you'll have to ride into town and get Sheriff Toffee.

MOE: But, Paw, it's a twenty-mile ride into town.

MOSS: Never mind, Little Brother; I'll go. You just set yourself down here and have some of Hip Sang's good food. Hey, Hip Sang!

(*Cook enters.*)

HIP SANG: Yes, Missa Moss? You call Hip Sang?

MOSS: Hip Sang, pack me a lunch. I gotta ride into town and get the sheriff.

(*Cook bows, goes offstage, and returns immediately with a large filled sack.*)

MOSS: Thanks, Hip Sang (*Takes sack*). I'll bring Roy back, Paw. (*Moss leaves and returns immediately with the Sheriff.*)

MOSS: Hello, Paw, Hip Sang, I'm ready for some food. I'll tell ya, that long ride to town and back just plumb tuckered me out. (*He sits down and begins to eat.*)

SHERIFF: Ban, what's this Moss is tellin' me about rustlers?

BAN: Somebody got into the north pasture last night and made off with half the herd the Army had ordered. Little Moe discovered they were gone when he rode up there this morning.

SHERIFF: That's bad, Ban. We oughta round up a posse and go after 'em, but I doubt if I can get mor'n a dozen men. I guess I better send for some help.

BAN: Now, Roy, I don't want you bringing in hired guns or bounty hunters.

SHERIFF: I wasn't thinkin' of that, Ban. I was thinkin' of askin' some lawmen to help. I'll get right back to town and get telegrams off to Fatt Killon, Clarke Goodepants, and the Lone Stranger.

(*Blackout*)

SCENE 2

(At Indian Wells Station. In a cabin a lone masked man sits at a table. Sound of horse approaching, door opens. PRONTO enters, battered and beaten, shirtless, with a large, broken feather in his headband.)

PRONTO: How, Kemosabe?

LONE STRANGER: Pronto, old friend, what did you find out in town?

PRONTO: Me bring-um telegram to masked-man friend.

L. S.: Well, Pronto, old friend, read it to me.

PRONTO: Telegram say old friend Ban Cartwheel got-um trouble with rustlers. Old friend Sheriff Toffee want-um you to come help-um catch rustlers.

L. S.: Pronto, old friend, why are you so battered and beaten?

PRONTO: Townspeople all hate-um Indians.

L. S.: The townspeople did this to you?

PRONTO: Yes, Kemosabe.

L. S.: Well, old friend, we'll have to report this incident to the N Double AIP.

PRONTO: What N Double AIP mean, Kemosabe?

L. S.: The National Association for the Advancement of Indian People.

PRONTO: You good-um fellow, Kemosabe.

L. S.: Pronto, old friend, because you and I have been friends for a long time now, don't you think you could tell me what "Kemosabe" means?

PRONTO: Kemosabe means Indian feller too chicken to fight white man.

(*Sound of many Indians offstage—in distance*)

L. S.: Pronto, that sounds like Geronimo and his braves have jumped the reservation and are headed this way.

PRONTO (*goes to window*): Me see Apaches now. They come from that-a-way. (*Points out window to right.*)

L. S. (*looks out door*): No, Pronto, they're coming from that-a-way. (*Points in opposite direction.*)

PRONTO: Kemosabe, me think-um Indians all around.

L. S.: Yes, Pronto, old friend, we are surrounded. It looks like this is the end of us.

PRONTO (*drawing tomahawk and starting toward* L. S.): What you mean us, paleface? (Pronto *chases* L. S. *offstage.*)

(*Blackout*)

SCENE 3

(In the marshal's office in Dodge City. MARSHAL KILLON sits at a table looking over some "wanted" circulars. CHASTER enters with telegram in hand.)

CHASTER: Mr. Killon, you gotta come quick. Doc is lyin' in the street with an arrow in his neck.

MARSHAL: Oh, hello, Chaster, What's that you got in your hand?

CHASTER: Huh? Oh, this here's a telegram. But you gotta come quick, Mr. Killon. Doc, he's lyin' in the street, and he's got an arrow in his neck!

MARSHAL: Now calm down, Chaster. Let's see what the telegram says.

CHASTER: But Mr. Kill . . . (KILLON *rises, takes telegram from* CHASTER, *sits back down to read.*)

MARSHAL: Hmm. Seems that Sheriff Toffee in Virginia City needs some help in rounding up some rustlers, Hmmm.

CHASTER: But, Mr. Killon, Doc's outside . . .

MARSHAL: Chaster, can't you be quiet a minute?

CHASTER: But, Mr. Killon, Doc's yore best friend, and you're just gonna sit there and let him die!

MARSHAL: Hmm. What you say, Chaster? What about Doc?

CHASTER: I been tryin' to tell you, Mr. Killon, but you just won't pay no 'tention to me. I just might as well not be here.

(*Enter* KATTY)

KATTY: Hello, Chaster. Hello, Fatt. Are you busy?

MARSHAL (*Standing as* KATTY *enters*): Why, no, Katty. What are you doing out this time of day?

KATTY: Well, it's such a nice day, I thought you might like to ride out on the prairie with me.

MARSHAL: Well, now, Katty, that sounds like a good idea.

KATTY: Say, Fatt, did you know Doc was lying out in the street with an arrow in his neck?

CHASTER: Yes, Mr. Killon, I been tryin' to tell you that.

MARSHAL: Now, Chaster, calm down. What're you tryin' to tell me about Doc?

CHASTER: Why, Mr. Killon, he's lyin' out thar in the street. He's got an arrow in his neck, and he's a-dyin'.

MARSHAL: Now, Chaster, you're just excited. Why don't you go out there and take another look?

(CHASTER *leaves and comes back in.*)

CHASTER: It's Doc, all right. And he's got an arrow in his neck, and he's dyin'.

(MARSHAL KILLON *pays no attention to him, but goes back to reading the telegram.*)

CHASTER: A fine friend you are, Mr. Killon. There yore best friend is out in the street with an arrow in his neck, and you just sit in here a-lookin' at some ol' telegram.

MARSHAL: What are you mumbling about, Chaster?

CHASTER: Mr. Killon, Doc's a-lyin' out thar in the street with an arrow in his neck.

MARSHAL: What! Doc? An arrow in his heart?

CHASTER: No, Mr. Killon; he got an arrow in his neck.

MARSHAL: Well, don't just stand there, Chaster. Go to the telegraph office and send Sheriff Toffee a telegram that I can't come just now because Doc's got an arrow in his foot. Then you get Doc out of the street and bring him in here. We gotta get that arrow out of his back!

CHASTER (*leaving*): Mr. Killon, it's in his neck!

MARSHAL: Never mind, Chaster; get a move on!

(*Blackout*)

SCENE 4

(*Inside the Silver Dollar Saloon.* CLARKE GOODEPANTS *sits at a table.*)

WAITER (*taking a drink over to table*): Here's yore sasaparilly, Mr. Goodepants. Say, you shore did a good job of running Dirty John an' his gang out of town.

GOODY: 'Twarn't nothin'.

(*Enter* LORETTA LOUISE, *who runs over to* GOODY.)

LORETTA: Oh, Clarke, honey, you're back! And you're safe! You're just the bravest man in the West! You've saved our town!

GOODY: 'Twarn't nothin'.

WAITER: Tell us how you did it, Mr. Goodepants.

GOODY: 'Twarn't nothin'.

(*Enter* TELEGRAPH CLERK *with telegram in hand.*)

CLERK: Mr. Goodepants, a message just come for you. It's

from Sheriff Toffee in Virginia City. Somebody stole seven hundred head of Ban Cartwheel's prize cattle, and they need your help to catch the rustlers.

(*Sound of horse approaching offstage, and a loud, "Whoa, horse!"*)

WAITER (*horrified*): Oh, that sounds like Deadeye Dick!

(LORETTA LOUISE *emits a scream and faints into* CLERK'S *arms.*)

DEADEYE (*offstage*): Whoa, horse! (*Horse continues to run.*) Aw, come on, horse, Whoa! (*Horse stops with screeching-of-brakes sound.*) (DEADEYE *clomps to door, steps just inside, and fires gun into air.*)

DEADEYE: Mah name is Deadeye, and ah'm a-lookin' for (*pulling paper out of pocket to check name*) Clarke Goody-pants. (*He does a double take at audience, says, "Good-y-pants?" and bursts out laughing.*)

WAITER (*stammering*): Mr. Deadeye, his name is Good-pants, not Good-y-pants; and it makes him powerful mad for somebody to call him Good-y-pants.

DEADEYE: Wal, that suits me jus' fine! Cause ah'm gonna blow him into little pieces. (*He raises his gun and fires at the ceiling.*)

(*During all this action,* GOODY *sups his drink as if nothing were happening. He ignores everything going on.*)

WAITER: Mr. Goodepants, didja hear him? Deadeye says he's gonna blow you to little pieces. You gotta do something. Show us how you gunned down Dirty John and his gang. Stop this loudmouth right now!

DEADEYE: Just a cotton-pickin' minute, thar! Who's a loud-mouth? (*grabs the* Waiter *by the shirt front and brandishes his gun in the* WAITER'S *face.*)

WAITER (*cringing*): Now, Mr. Goodepants, Now!

(GOODY *is finishing his drink and pays no attention to* Deadeye. DEADEYE *suddenly turns the* WAITER *loose and levels his gun at* GOODY *to fire. Meanwhile* LORETTA *has revived, sees what is about to happen, and grabs* Deadeye's *arm. His shot goes wild.* GOODY *sets his glass down, adjusts his gun belt, draws his gun, and fires at* DEADEYE, *who staggers, wounded gravely.*)

DEADEYE: Oh, you got me! I'm at the end of my rope! (*He sings "The Last Roundup" and "O bury me not on the lone prairie, where the coyotes howl and the wind blows free."*) But I ain't goin' alone! (*He fires at* GOODY *just as he hits the floor.*)

(GOODY *grabs his arm—not his shootin' hand—and slumps to the chair.*)

WAITER: Oh, Mr. Goodepants, you done it again! You killed that blabby outlaw. You're the biggest hero we ever had!

GOODY: 'Twarn't nuthin'.

WAITER: I'll call his horse, so we can take him to the doctor. (*Steps to door and calls, "Horse." Horse head appears in doorway.*)

WAITER: Miss Loretta, you're a hero, too. You saved Mr. Goodepants. (*He turns to* GOODY.) Why don't you give Miss Loretta a great big kiss?

GOODY (*drawing himself up to his full height*): My mother brought me up to be a right proper boy. I don't never kiss no one but my horse. (*He kisses the horse with a loud smack.*)

HORSE (*whinnies loudly and stamps feet*): Boy, you're right! 'Twarn't nuthin'.

(*Blackout*)

SCENE 5

(*Back on the* Proponderosa BAN, MOSS, and LITTLE MOE *are* sitting at a table eating. HIP SANG *serves. Sounds of horses approaching. Knock on door.* HIP SANG *opens door.* SHERIFF *enters.*)

SHERIFF: Ban, I got bad news. We're gonna have to go after them rustlers ourselves. The Lone Stranger's got Indian trouble, Marshal Killon can't leave Dodge because Doc's got an arrow in his neck, and Clarke Goodepants was wounded in a gunfight with Deadeye Dick. I've managed to round up a small posse, and we're starting out now. Little Moe, did you happen to notice which way the tracks led off?

LITTLE MOE: Yeah, Roy, they went toward the east.

MOSS: Roy. You ride on ahead. I'll join you after I finish eating.

BAN: Good luck, Roy.

(SHERIFF *exits.*)

(*Another knock on door.* HIP SANG *opens door.* SCHOOLMARM *enters.*)

BAN (*rising*): Well, good evening, Miss Sarah Beth. What brings you out to the Proponderosa?

MISS SARAH BETH: Hello, Mr. Cartwheel, Moss, Little Moe. (*She continues to look at* LITTLE MOE *though talking to* BAN.) I'm sorry to interrupt your dinner this way, but I was told that Sheriff Toffee was here.

BAN: You just come and sit down here, Miss Sarah Beth. Sheriff Toffee stopped by here, but he and the posse are out after the rustlers.

MOSS: What was it you wanted to see Sheriff Toffee about, Miss Sarah Beth? Maybe we could do something to help you.

MISS SARAH BETH: Well, I wanted to talk with the sheriff about a new boy at school; he's causing me some trouble. You see, he's really more a man than a boy, and I just can't seem to handle him.

MOE: Well, now, Miss Sarah Beth, maybe I can help you. Why don't I see you home, and you can tell me all about your problem? (*He takes her arm, and they leave.*)

MOSS: Hip Sang, I could use some more of this stew. (HIP SANG *goes out.*) Paw, you know, if I was gonna steal some cattle, I'd take 'em up on Ghost Mesa. I think I'll ride up . . .

(*Noise outside. Knock on door.* HIP SANG *returns on stage, puts dish down on table, and opens door.* SHERIFF *enters.*)

BAN: Roy, you're back!

SHERIFF: Yeah, Ban, we got 'em! Nabbed the whole gang comin' back for more of the herd. The posse's takin' 'em in to jail.

(*Noise outside.* HIP SANG *opens door.* MARSHAL KILLON *and* CHASTER *enter.*)

BAN: Why, Fatt Killon! I thought you were in Dodge City. (BAN *shakes hands with* KILLON *and* CHASTER.)

MARSHAL: We got the arrow out of Doc's neck, so Chaster and I came to help you catch the rustlers.

(*Noise outside.* HIP SANG *opens door.* CLARKE GOODEPANTS *and* LORETTA *enter.*)

SHERIFF: Why, Mr. Goodepants! And Miss Loretta!

BAN: Clarke, how good of you to come—even when you're hurt! You must tell us all about your showdown with Deadeye. (*He shakes hands with* GOODY *and* LORETTA.)

GOODY: 'Twarn't nuthin'.

(*Noise outside.* HIP SANG *opens door.* LONE STRANGER *and*

PRONTO *enter, arm in arm, singing "Kemosabe" to the tune of "Frere? Jacques." LITTLE MOE follows and makes third part of round.*)

BAN: Well, gentlemen, this makes our group complete! (*He shakes hands with LONE STRANGER and PRONTO.*)

L. S.: Ban Cartwheel, we come to help you.

BAN: I thought you were having trouble with Indians.

PRONTO: Me decide-um chasing rustlers more fun than chasing white man.

MOE: Say, why didn't someone tell me we were having a party?

BAN: Now that the rustlers have been safely put in jail, and everyone's here, we can have a party. (*They all sing to tune "Home on the Range."*)

> Oh, give me a home,
> Where the bad guys still roam,
> Where the sheriff's the hero each day.
> The bad guys you can tell,
> By the way that they smell,
> And I'll tell you they don't smell like hay!

> Home, home on the range,
> Where the good guys still wear white hats.
> Where the quick draw that's fast,
> Will be the cowboy that lasts,
> And being a bad guy don't pay.

> Oh, give me a home
> Where the deacons don't roam
> Where the preacher's the good guy each
> day.
> Where a bad show like this

Never got booed or hissed,
'Cause the audience slept through the play.

Home, home on the range
At (*name of church*) these actors did play.
And sometimes we heard a discouraging word,
But we know you still love us the same,
But we know you still love us the same.

The Barn Party

This is an evening of fun, based on an old-fashioned barn party theme. Use plenty of imagination. Involve lots of people and have a good time!

CHARACTERS

MASTER OF CEREMONIES
DOTTIE PARDON
PIGGY MAE
MISS PRUNELLA GOODBODY
MISS RITA LORETTA
LADY #1
LADY #2
THE GREASY GAP BREAKDOWN BAND
GRAMPA
MAN
LADY #3
THE CHAWIN' GUMM SANGERS
YOUTH LEADER OR DIRECTOR

SETTING

A barn is a perfect place for the party. A storeroom or a warehouse would be good, but don't despair, since a fellowship hall or gymnasium can be used.

PROPS

a few bales of hay, jugs, and kitchen utensils for the band
bell
tape recording of female vocalist
tape player
wig

MC: Welcome, ladies and gentlemen, to the (*name of your church*) barn party. We want you to relax and really enjoy the show. Our fabulous show is sponsored by none other than that favorite of all chawing gums, Peerless Gum! (THE CHAWIN' GUMM SANGERS *begin to sing, then hum behind the* MC. *They could do this with each commercial.*) Throughout this evening you will hear from some satisfied customers of Peerless Gum. So here with our first unsolicited testimonial is Miss Piggy Mae. Give her a hand, folks!

PIGGY: Yes, well, I just love Peerless. I mend my false teeth with it. I mean there ain't any chaw like it. See what it did for my smile! (*She smiles, and part of her teeth are missing--black 'em out.*)

MC: Thank you, Miss Piggy Mae! And remember, folks, Peerless comes in three delicious flavors: licorice, persimmon, pistachio, and the new tutti fruiti flavor!
There's a special guest with us tonight. Miss Prunella Goodbody. She has been sent here to make sure that we have a clean show. Miss Goodbody will let us know if any part of the show is getting out of line. When you hear her ring her little bell, that will be our warning. Ring your little bell, Miss Goodbody. (*She rings bell vigorously . . . she will be on her own the entire evening. She should ring her bell and interrupt at even the slightest hint of misdemeanor.*)

MC: And now our first guest! We are privileged to start off the entertainment tonight with one of the legends of country music, Miss Rita Loretta.

(Miss Rita Loretta *lip-syncs to tape*)

MC: Wasn't that wonderful, folks? Let's really hear it for Miss Rita Loretta! (*After applause has died down*) And now our next unsolicited testimony for our sponsor, Peerless Gum.

Lady #1: Well, I use Peerless like putty and crack filler around the house. Of coursin', I have to chaw a case of thet gum fer the best results. I even use it to clean my glasses. (*She turns to go off and runs into wall or* MC *or other objects.*)

MC: We've got time for another one. . . . Yes, you, Sir. Tell us what Peerless has done for you?

Lady #2 (*made up to have bad complexion*) Well, I had always chawed Peerless Gum, and I heard tell of a woman who had bad problems with her skin, so she started puttin' (sic-*pronounced like what you do on a golf green*) the gum all over her skin. I heard tell that some women uses mud and cucumbers and even them green pears from Mexico, so I started sticking Peerless Gum all over myself. *And lo and behold!* Look hyar at my face. Ain't it radiant? Jest like them models on TV. I keep Peerless with me all the time. Coursin, Jed—he's my husband—had to move out of the house into the barn 'cause there ain't no room for any thang else but me and my Peerless Gum.

MC: That is truly amazing! Just look at her adorable face. Thank you, Ma'am, for sharing this miracle with us. And now . . . our very own . . . the Greasy Gap Breakdown Band!

(The Greasy Gap Breakdown Band *hams it up with a director, soloists, etc.*)

MC: Well, thank you. That was interesting! Now our next guest is a most unusual person. Grampa is 112 years old. Now, folks, you'd never believe it, but he is. Welcome, Grampa! Grampa, it's just great to see you again. But I'm surprised you're here. I thought you were in the Alps doing some skiing.

GRAMPA: Oh, Son, I've been back from skiing for a spell now.

MC: Then what have you been up to lately?

GRAMPA: Skydiving! I've been skydiving lately.

MC: That sounds dangerous. Tell me about it?

GRAMPA: We were up in the air about 10,000 feet, and we were getting ready to jump. The instructor told me to jump. But I said I'd better wait 'til I get a little older.

MC: That's probably best, Grampa. So you didn't jump after all?

GRAMPA: No I jumped.

MC: Oh, what made you change your mind?

GRAMPA: The instructor.

MC: What did he say to convince you to jump?

GRAMPA: He didn't say nothin'. He pushed me!

MC: Oh, that's bad.

GRAMPA: No, that's good. I enjoyed it for a while.

MC: Oh, that's good.

GRAMPA: No, that's bad! My parachute wouldn't open.

MC: Oh, now that's bad!

GRAMPA: No, that's good. I spotted a haystack, and I was headed for it.

MC: Well, that's good.

GRAMPA: No, that's bad. The haystack had a pitchfork in it.

MC: That's bad.

GRAMPA: No, I missed the pitchfork.
MC: That's good.

GRAMPA: No, that's bad. When I landed, I missed the haystack and broke my leg.

MC: Now, I know that's bad!

GRAMPA: Oh no, that's good! See, they took me to the hospital, and I had the prettiest nurse you ever saw.

MC: Oooh, that's good!

GRAMPA: No, that's bad! My girlfriend caught me flirting with the nurse, and she said she'd never speak to me again.

MC: That is bad!

GRAMPA: What did you say?

MC: I said, that's bad.

GRAMPA: You got that wrong, Friend! That's good, I mean real good. You don't know my girlfriend. I mean she'd talk the ears off a stalk of corn. And she's got a bad case of the "uglies." She's so ugly, I mean, she's so ugly that she has to sneak up on a glass of water to get a drink. She's so ugly, pimples are afraid to get on her face. (*He goes off muttering.*) That's good, my Friend, real good . . .

MC: Thank you, Grampa, for this tremendous enlightenment. That was good . . . er . . . whatever. And now here's a word from our sponsor, Peerless Gum, that's as mild and tasty as the new-mown hay. Ah, here's a gent with an unsolicited testimony. Yes, you Sir, how long have you been chewing Peerless?

MAN #2: Yep, I'm only fifty-seven years old, and if I don't have my gum first thang in the morning I feel much older.

So, I don't miss my morning chaw because it helps my headaches and that rundown feeling. But my main trouble is centered on my wooden leg—I found that it was slowly rotting away. It was a happy day when (*name of any well-liked lady in the church or group*) told me about good old Peerless and what it had done in her life. Thanks to Peerless, new life has come into me. No longer do I fear the rotting of my wooden leg! In fact, I now have to carry pruning shears with me to keep the sprouts from a-growin'.

MC: Thank you, Sir. Now who will be next?

LADY #3: I'll give my testimony. Our church was having trouble getting people to come to our Sunday night services and training programs. We tried everythang. So we took our problems to (*pastor's name*). He suggested that we chew Peerlesss like he does. So we laid in a stock of good, ole Peerless, the chew that's made for you. Now, we ain't got room for everybody. After our great success, all the church programs started using Peerless, even the ladies' organization, but the choir did have to quit using it in choir practice. The front row kept getting their bubbles all over (*name of music director*).

MC: Thank you for that inspiring word! Now let's bring out the Chawin' Gumm Sangers agin.
Songs for the Chawin' Gumm Sangers

(*to the tune of "She'll Be Comin' Round the Mountain"*)
She'll be coming round the mountain when she comes,
She'll be coming round the mountain when she comes,
She'll be coming round the mountain,

She'll be coming round the mountain,
She'll be coming round the mountain when she
comes.

She'll be chawin' Peerless Gum when she comes,
She'll be chawin' Peerless Gum when she comes,
She'll be chawin' Peerless Gum,
She'll be chawin' Peerless Gum,
She'll be chawin' Peerless Gum when she comes.

(*to the tune of "Home, Home on the Range"*)
Chaw, chaw in yore jaw,
It's Peerless, the gum for you.
Chewers find it's so dandy,
And it's 'bout gooder than candy,
So try it, and you'll chaw it too.

MC: Thank you . . . that was . . . interesting. And now the big
moment we've all been waiting for! Now, I will have to ask
all of you men to sit down through the next guest's appear-
ance on our show. Not only is she pretty as a newborn calf,
but she can sing, too! Give a warm welcome to Miss Dottie
Pardon!

(*Everyone cheers wildly*—MISS GOODBODY *rings her bell
frantically.*)

MC: Welcome to the show. Miss Pardon, how are you?

DOTTIE: Can't you tell?

MC: Oh, yes, I mean, uh, Miss Pardon.

DOTTIE: Please, anyone as cute as you can call me Dottie.

MC: Uh, yes, Dottie. Well, Dottie, it is obvious that the men
really like you. Why, old men act like they were kids again.

DOTTIE: Well, I'm real pleased that the men like me, but it does have its drawbacks.

MC: Oh? And how's that?

DOTTIE: Well, just awhile ago someone tried to kiss me outside the stage—in the dark. But I did manage to bite his hand real hard. I'm pretty sure I brought blood.

MC (*horrified*): Dottie, I'm so sorry this has happened. We ask your forgiveness for this horrible act.

YOUTH LEADER or DIRECTOR (*enters and interrupts*): I hate to interrupt the show, but I feel that this must be dealt with right now. First, I have to say that I am real disappointed at someone in this group. This could be the only thing that Miss Pardon remembers about our church. Or, it could be the only thing she remembers about the whole town of (*your town*). That some degenerate tried to kiss her right here at our barn party. I am really upset! So, that person—and you know who you are—needs to meet me immediately after the show. Really, I am so disappointed! (*During this talk,* YOUTH LEADER *makes sure everyone can see his hand. It is bandaged and has blood stains on the bandage.*)

MC: I can see why he is so upset. We truly hope you will forgive us for this terrible thing that has happened.

DOTTIE: Ah, there's no harm done.

MC: Dottie, you are so gracious. Would you sing for us now?

DOTTIE: Sure . . . (DOTTIE *lip-syncs to a different female country-western recording than that of* MISS RITA LORETTA.)

MC: Thank you, let's hear it for all our talent for tonight . . . (*applause, all come back on stage*) . . . now do we have one more testimony?

(*End the evening with a serious testimony, then sing a hymn such as "Amazing Grace" or other well-known hymn, as many country and western shows are often concluded.*)

MIKE PEARCE, the author of *The Barn Party,* is minister of recreation at the First Baptist Church of Huntsville, Alabama.

Love Through the Ages

This is a drama in rhyme. It can be done easily with narrator, little dialogue, and little rehearsal. The actors do the actions as the piece is read. Costuming is important.

CHARACTERS

SAMSON AND DELILAH
MARIAN AND ROBIN HOOD
ROMEO AND JULIET
NAPOLEON AND JOSEPHINE
STARLETT AND RHITT
BONEY AND CLOYDE
MA AND PA KITTLE
MALE AND FEMALE HIPPIES
NARRATOR

PROPS

wig

NARRATOR: It all came about from Heaven above
   because God made man want to love and be loved.
   And so we present without a rehearse
   our love story characters   for better or worse.

SCENE 1

(*Characters may begin a tableau that is added to at the end of each scene or characters may exit after each scene.*)

45

(SAMSON AND DELILAH *enter.*)

NARRATOR: Then there was mighty Samson, with his long, flowing hair,
> and he met Delilah, a maiden so fair.
> Where he got his strength she determined to find,
> so she gave him some kissin' that drove him plain blind

(*Couple to act out scene.*)

> The end of this story by Samson is said,

SAMSON: Don't trust a woman whatever you dare,
> Don't trust a woman,
> Or you might lose your hair! (*He takes off wig.*)

SCENE 2

(MAID MARIAN *enters.*)

NARRATOR: Maid Marian sat on a stump one day,
> and with a stick began to play.
> She drew a heart in the dirt, then whined,

MAID MARIAN: But who would be my Valentine?

NARRATOR: She thought of all the fellows that could,
> and then she said,

MAID MARIAN: I'll bet . . .

(*Robin jumps on stage.*)

ROBIN: Robin would!

SCENE 3

(ROMEO *and* JULIET *enter.*)

NARRATOR: Our very next couple was love's greatest pair,
> their love was filled with war and despair,
> So hear for yourself from the lovers we've met:

JULIET (*sobs loudly into her handkerchief*): "Oh, Romeo,

Romeo!''

ROMEO: Do you think it could be something
    that Juli - et?

SCENE 4

(NAPOLEON *and* JOSEPHINE *enter.*)

NARRATOR: A pair of lovers who caused much ado,
    was Napoleon and Josephine, before Waterloo.
    He gave her big rubies and diamonds and pearls,
    while she spent her time arranging her curls.
    The reason she married him I understand
    Was to get back her teeth that he held in his hand.

(JOSEPHINE *tries to pull* NAPOLEON'S *hand from his coat.*)

SCENE 5

(STARLETT *and* RHITT *enter.*)

NARRATOR: Starlett, the beauty, and Rhitt, the man about
town,
    had a love between them whose fire knew no bounds.
    Through the anger and passion of the great Civil War,
    Their anger and passion were even much more.
    So we let Rhitt give his famous last line,

RHITT: Frankly, Starlett, I don't give Valentines!

SCENE 6

(BONEY *and* CLOYDE *enter.*)

NARRATOR: Wild through the midwest these lovers did ride,
    Always together, side by side.
    He went to the banks with his lady fair,
    and helped himself to the money there.
    To murder and steal seemed to fill them with pride.

CLOYDE: You're my Boney.

BONEY: You're my Cloyde.

SCENE 7

(MA *and* PA KITTLE *enter.*)

NARRATOR: They are no youngsters, they're fit as a fiddle,
The couple of lovers known as Ma and Pa Kittle.

MA: Be bright and chipper if you want fame.

NARRATOR: But slow and lazy was his game.
The reason they were married is because, long ago,
when the preacher said, "Do you?" he was slow saying no.

SCENE 8

(TWO HIPPIES--ONE MALE, ONE FEMALE)

NARRATOR: And then the hippies came on the scene
and it seemed that "love" was really their theme.
Love came to light as seldom before,
"Make love," they cried, "instead of war."
Long hair, short skirts, long coats and pants,
ruffled shirts, bell bottoms and no shoes,
gave no chance
To tell fellows from the ladies fair, unless they
told you . . .

MALE: I'm a boy!

FEMALE: I'm a girl!

SCENE 9

NARRATOR: Now rock and roll is the theme.
Once it was simple, now extreme.
Love's still there but with a beat,
If you don't have it, please retreat.
Hard to recognize, hard to see,
But the same as ever, love's to be

Strong, real, and wonderful.
For with rock and roll, love's never dull.

(*Couple enters, claps hands as to a beat. They embrace.*)

The moral to our story is plain as can be,
One that each one here can see;
We can live in the future or dwell in the past,
But one thing for certain, love's gonna last!

This drama was written by JO—MRS. JIM—BYRNE, First Baptist Church, Hot Springs, Arkansas, who has granted permission for its use.

"The Evening Show"

This is a spoof of the famous TV show, "The Tonight Show." Using people who resemble the real celebrities adds to the fun.

CHARACTERS

TED MCHANAN: *announcer*
MAC LEVERENSON: *band leader*
CONNIE JARSON: *host*
ANGELINA CONRAD: *guest (150 years old)*
JOE JOCK: *guest (super athlete)*
AUDIENCE *(Plant some people in the audience as needed. Add as many guests as you like. You could lengthen this skit to make an evening-length program.)*

PROPS

can with made-up dog food label
dog dish
real dog or a toy dog
envelopes and three-by-five cards
jug (to be played)
tape and tape player or pianist

TED: And welcome to "The Evening Show," starring Connie Jarson. And herrrrrrrrrre's Connie! *(Wild applause)*

CONNIE *(bows to audience . . . touches nose . . . rubs hands together . . . smiles toward band, etc.)*: I can see that you're a

50

good group. Now, the audience we had last evening, well, I hate to speak evil of the dead, but-- they were really a tough audience.

AUDIENCE: How tough were they?

CONNIE: Well, I'll tell you how tough they were. They were so tough, they'd make Dracula look like Mother Teresa. Now folks, that's tough! But there was this little old lady who liked the show. She came backstage and gave me a lemon cream pie . . . right in the face. But I can tell, you folks aren't like that. In fact, the group was so bad last evening we had some special seats installed in the audience. They are all wired so that if you don't laugh at the jokes, you'll get a shock. But, seriously, Folks, did you read about the big fire at the shoe factory? Oh, it was big! Over a thousand soles were lost. (*If group groans, host will remind them about the electrically wired seats.*)

(*Looking at band*) Hello, Mac, it's good of you to be here this evening. Mac does so many concerts and opening of malls it's a privilege to have him here. (MAC *is dressed in extremely loud clothing and holds a trumpet.*) I hear your concerts are being sold out.

MAC: Yeah, I probably won't need this job much longer, Boss Man!

CONNIE: What a wit! Always kidding! If you get bigger laughs than I do, you may leave sooner than you think.

(CONNIE *turns to* TED.)

TED: And who are our guests this evening, Big Fellow?

CONNIE: We have a great lineup this evening on "The Evening Show."

TED: We are waiting with baited breath, Sir Jarson.

CONNIE: That's not the kind of breath you usually wait with!

Oh, yes, our guests. There's Angelina Conrad. Angelina is 150 years old. The oldest jug player (*and anything else*) in the world. Angelina will play her famous rendition of Suwannee River for us this evening. And we have the winner of the Super Jock of the World Award with us: Joe Jock. Joe is the number-one draft pick of the NFL, NBA, and NHL. We'll talk to Joe about what he really wants to do with his life. But now a word from our sponsor. Don't go away, we'll be right back (*does golf swing.*).

(*The commercial involves* TED *and a dog. This can be done with a live dog or a stuffed dog. The latter may be easier to handle.*)

TED: Here we see man's best friend. How are you tonight, Bowser? If you really love your dog, as I love Bowser, you'll feed him what's best for him, Yalpo. The best for the best! (*Sets dish down in front of dog.*) See how Bowser loves Yalpo? Get Yalpo for your best friend. I'm sure he will love it as much as Bowser does. (*Dog does not eat food.*)

(*Brief blackout*)

TED: This evening we have a very special guest with us from the East. The great seer, soothsayer, and borderline mystic. Welcome Jarsoni the Magnificent!

(*The great* PARSONI *enters. He is dressed in a huge jeweled turban and a cape over his regular clothing. He stumbles as he walks to the desk and is seated.*)

TED: Great Parsoni, we have here the envelopes. Inside these envelopes are questions, never having been seen by you. These envelopes have been hermetically sealed in a mayonnaise jar and kept on the porch of Funk and Wagnalls. No one . . . *no one* . . . has seen them until now. But you, in your amazing manner, will, in some mysterious fashion, give the answer to these questions, without ever seeing the question. The first envelope . . .

CONNIE: May the bird of paradise roost in your attic during molting season.

(*You may wish to insert your answers and questions here. These could be about local people or incidents. The following are some examples.*)

CONNIE (*holds envelope to head*): Singing in the drain.

TED: Singing in the drain.

CONNIE: What was Gene Kelly singing as he was being washed down the sewer?

TED: The next envelope, Brilliant One.

CONNIE (*as before*): Tick-Tock.

TED: Tick-Tock.

CONNIE: If the big hand of the clock is on eight and the little hand is at three, what does the clock say?

(TED *hands* CONNIE *the next envelope.*)

CONNIE: The fatted calf.

TED: The fatted calf.

CONNIE (*opens envelope*): Who was sorry when the prodigal son returned?

(*Next envelope*)

CONNIE: Bowwow.

TED: Bowwow.

CONNIE (*as he opens envelope*): There must be an echo in here. The question is: What is a spot announcement?

(*Next envelope)*

TED: And now, O Potentate, here is the last envelope.

(AUDIENCE *applauds wildly*).

CONNIE: May the bird of paradise sing joyful songs at your funeral. . . . The answer is . . . General Electric.

TED: General Electric.

CONNIE: What is the name of the man in charge of the power plant?

(CONNIE *rises to leave as* TED *says good-bye, O Sage, etc.*)

TED (*to* AUDIENCE): Let's give a big hand to Jarsoni the Magnificent!

(*Insert something of a local interest or another Yalpo commercial here.*)

(CONNIE *returns minus turban and cape.*)

CONNIE: Our first guest this evening is 150 years old. Her name is Angelina Conrad. Angelina comes from right here in Hollywood. . . . She's still here, isn't she? We wanted to be sure to get Angelina on first, for obvious reasons.

(ANGELINA *comes in. She's old, but spry. She is carrying a brown jug. She sits in chair, won't let* TED *have her jug. Sits and glares at* CONNIE.)

CONNIE: Miss Conrad, may I call you Angelina?

ANGELINA: Yes, but remember, just because I'm old you can't take advantage of me!

CONNIE: I wouldn't do that!

ANGELINA: Well, I've heard about you Hollywood types; any pretty face is in danger.

CONNIE: Now, Angelina, just relax; we're all your friends.

ANGELINA: Tell your humongous friend to stay away from me and my musical instrument.

CONNIE: He's just trying to help you.

ANGELINA: Well, this jug is a finely tuned instrument, and I don't want any fingerprints on it!

CONNIE: Speaking of the jug, why don't you play a tune for us?

ANGELINA: I thought you'd never ask! (*She stands. Makes a great fuss about getting the jug just right, etc.*)

ANGELINA: OK, Mac, hit it! (*Play tape or have pianist accompany the jug player. The better she plays the jug the funnier it will be.*)

CONNIE: My, that was interesting. Angelina, do you get many opportunities to perform?

ANGELINA: Yes, all the time. They love me at the Home. Most of those dummies can't hear too good anyway.

CONNIE: Well, Angelina, it's been good to have you with us this evening.

(TED *gets up to help* ANGELINA *off stage*)

ANGELINA: I'm not ready to go yet. Are you trying to get rid of me?

CONNIE: Of course not, Angelina, but isn't this a little past your bedtime? Ted will help you find your way out.

ANGELINA: I don't need any help! Get your hands off me! (*She struggles all the way off the stage.*)

CONNIE: That was an experience! Now to our next guest. Joe has won every possible award. There seems to be nothing left, in the area of sports for him to conquer. Let's welcome Joe Jock, super athlete of the world!

(JOE *comes in to wild applause. He raises his hands over his head in a victory pose, does a high five with* CONNIE, *does a celebration dance, and finally sits down.*)

CONNIE: Well, Joe, how does it feel to be *super jock of the world*?

JOE (*speaks hesitantly, with lots of uh's, yah know's, know what I mean, and right*): Good, Mr. Jarson, real good.

CONNIE: What do you think of the draft, Joe?

JOE: Oh, that's all right, Mr. Jarson, I don't get cold too easy!

CONNIE: No, Joe the NFL, NBA, and NHL drafts?

JOE: Uh, well it's OK, Mr. Jarson.

CONNIE: Just OK, Joe? You'll be offered a zillion dollars to sign with any team. What else is there you could possibly want to do?

JOE: Well, uh, Mr. Jarson.

CONNIE: Yes, Joe.

JOE: Well, uh, Mr. Jarson, I've always wanted to do one of those jock commercials . . . you know, the ones where the sports person sells something.

CONNIE: Why Joe, I believe we can make that wish of yours come true . . . would you really like that?

JOE: Oh, Mr. Jarson, it would make me the happiest jock in the world!

CONNIE: Well, OK, Joe . . . see that TV prompter over there . . .

JOE: Yeah . . .

CONNIE: You just read what it says there, and you'll be doing a jock commercial.

JOE: OK. . . Mr. Jarson! (*He squints as he reads.* TED *hands him a razor.* JOE *points to his chin.*) Ya' see all these little hairs on my face . . . well, I just shaved my face on this side, and there ain't no hairs left . . . I mean there ain't no hairs left anywhere on mah face . . . I mean, you see, if I use this credit card on the side I shaved, you can't hear nothin' cause there ain't nothing there . . . no little hairs or nothin'.

CONNIE (*interrupting*): Joe, I think that will be just fine. You have done just fine ... (*continues to assure him as he rushes him off the stage.*)

(*To* TED) Ted, call the sponsor, apologize to him. See if we are still on the air . . . (*To* AUDIENCE) That's all for this evening folks. . . . Tune in (*I hope*) tomorrow evening for another fun-filled "Evening Show!"

(*Black out*)

The Famous Couples' Banquet

SAMSON and DELILAH
ROMEO and JULIET
MISS KATTY and FATT KILLON with GUNSLINGER SAM
JULY CARTER and LONNIE CASH
THE MOST FAMOUS PAIRS of ALL (*see* PROPS)
(*All characters are dressed in keeping with the time in history, such as* SAMSON *being dressed in biblical dress.*)

PROPS

sofa or bed
ladder for balcony
toy guns (or use fingers and pretend)
country music tape with male and female singers
tape player
slides: Two or more months before this program, take slides of couples in your church. A good time is immediately following the morning worship service since most everyone is dressed up. Gather information from these couples, such as the title of "their song" when they were dating or something pertaining to their meeting or courtship that would be good material for the program.

ANNOUNCER: To celebrate the Valentine season, we bring you,

at practically no expense, the real story of several famous pairs. You have heard of these people or read about them in history. Right here for the very first time, we bring you the facts. Our experts have spent months, weeks, days (well, a few minutes), to bring this incredible program to you. We begin with the real facts about Samson and Delilah.

SCENE 1

SAMSON: Dee, I'd like to take a nap, but I don't trust you.

DELILAH: Why, Sammy, love, how could that be? What have I done to make you distrust me?

SAMSON: Oh, nothing much! You asked me, "Wherein does your strength lie?" and I answered: "Bind me with seven green twigs that were never dried. Then I shall be as weak as another man." Then the Philistines came, and I broke the twigs easily.

You asked me again to tell you the secret of my strength. I told you to bind me with new ropes. Then the Philistines came, and once again I broke free.

You asked me again, and I said, "Braid my hair." The Philistines came, and I was still strong.

DELILAH: Just coincidences! Sammy, by the way, wherein does your strength lie?

SAMSON: Oh, no, you don't!

DELILAH (*running her fingers through his hair*): Sammy, you hurt my feelings!

SAMSON: Will you quit that? (*removing her fingers from his hair*). You're messing with my strength. (*He realizes what he has said, and puts his hand over his mouth.*)

DELILAH (*aside*): Oh, ho! No wonder he's so vain about his hair! That's it! (Delilah *holds up scissors and smiles.*)

(*Blackout*)

SCENE 2

(*Famous balcony scene from* Romeo and Juliet. JULIET *stands on balcony and speaks.*)

JULIET: Romeo, Romeo, wherefore art thou, Romeo?

ROMEO (*dressed in overalls, answers with hillbilly accent*): Right-cheer, Juliet. What do you want, Honey?

JULIET: Oh, well, I'll try again tomorrow night.

(*Blackout*)

SCENE 3

FATT (*at desk, to himself*): Sure is a lot of rustlin' goin' on in these parts. Look at all these wanted posters! Guess I gotta stir myself to get out and round 'em up. (*He gets up from desk as* MISS KATTY *comes in.*)

MISS KATTY: Fatt, I'm glad I found you in. It's such a nice day. Let's go for a ride on the prairie.

FATT: Miss Katty, there's nothin' I'd like better, but I've gotta round up these rustlers.

MISS KATTY: Oh, Fatt, you can round up rustlers anytime (*coyly*), but you can't go for a ride with me just anytime!

FATT: Well, you know, Miss Katty, you're right, let's go!

(*Enter* GUNSLINGER SAM)

SAM: Hold it! Just hold it one minute! I have come to challenge you, Fatt Killon, to a shootout! You think you're such a good shot, smart-aleck sheriff! I can beat you anytime. Come on, draw!

FATT (*backing off*): Now wait a minute, Sam. I can't have a shootout here. Miss Katty is too delicate and ladylike to see anything like that!

SAM: I don't care, Mister Killon, we're gonna prove right now who's the best shot in the West.

FATT (*begging*): Now, Sam, we can settle this later . . .

SAM: No! Right now!

(*He backs up.* KILLON *backs up. They face each other.* KATTY *slips behind* FATT. *She draws as* FATT *draws. A shot rings out.* SAM *grabs his shoulder,* FATT *looks stunned.*)

SAM: Why you dirty lawman, you shot me!

(*They both look at* KATTY, *who pretends to blow smoke from her gun.*)

MISS KATTY: Now, we know who's the best shot in the West. Ready for that ride, Fatt?

(*Blackout*)

SCENE 4

ANNOUNCER: And now to sing for us, that famous couple, July Carter and Lonnie Cash.
(JULY CARTER *and* LONNIE CASH *lip-sync a country duet.*)

SCENE 5

ANNOUNCER: You have seen and heard from famous pairs of the past. Now, we have our own famous pairs. (*Using material gathered earlier, let actors act out the stories of the courtships of several couples as you show their slides. Use music suitable to that particular time. Select couples from the thirties, forties, etc., and a newlywed couple. Close with Scripture reading from Genesis 1:26-27; 2:21-24.*)

First Annual Lemmy Awards

The "Lemmy Awards" is a program most effectively used about the time of the annual Emmy awards. The Emmy is given for the best TV performances of the year. The "Lemmy" is given for the worst performances of the year.

CHARACTERS

MASTER OF CEREMONIES
STELLA STARLET
LONUS
OLIVE FIG-NEWTON JOHN
ROCKY ROADS
JANE
LUCY
POLICEMAN
DAVEY DOG AND THE BOW-WOW-WOWS

PROPS

envelopes with cards inside
blanket
music for OLIVE FIG-NEWTON JOHN, for the soap-opera scene
and silverware
box of tissues

MC: Ladies and Gentlemen, welcome to the first annual "Lemmy Awards" show. Tonight, right here on this stage, you will see the best of the worst—yes, "Lemmy" awards for the worst TV performances of the year. And now to present the nominees for the worst documentary of the year is Stella Starlet. Give her a big hand!

(STELLA *makes her entrance—and makes the most of it.*)

MC (*a little irritated*): Uh, Miss Starlet, will you read the nominations, please?

STELLA: Oh, yes, thank you. And the nominations are - "Rock Snakes and Their Habitat," starring Chuckie Brown; "Macrame Is Life," starring Robert Blueford; and "Of Male and Female," with Barbara Whatsit (*opens envelope*). And the winner is - "Rock Snakes and Their Habitat!" And acccepting for Chuckie Brown is Lonus!

LONUS (*makes his approach carrying blanket*): Thank you. Chuckie loves you! And remember Rock snakes can't hurt you much because they aren't very tall, and when they throw rocks, they can only hit you in the leg. Thank you!

MC: Thank you, Lonus. And we'll remember about the Rock Snakes. Now for a change of pace—one of the songs nominated for the worst song heard on TV this year, as sung by Olive Fig-Newton John.

(OLIVE FIG-NEWTON JOHN *lip-syncs to any song, sung badly, or a parody.*)

MC: Wow! Great! Worst song I ever heard! And now to present the nominations for the worst daytime serial of the year is— that famous film star, Rocky Roads. Let's hear that applause! (*Someone should also be set up to boo and hiss occasionally.*)

(ROCKY *enters, hands clasped over his head.*)

ROCKY: Thank you, loyal fans. I do deserve every bit of your adoration! Keep it up! The nominations for the worst day-time serials are: "As the Stomach Growls," "Are These My Children?" and the "Nurse-amids." (*Opens the envelope.*) And the winner is: "As the Stomach Turns!" Here's a scene from this award-winning series.

(*Light comes up on scene of two women sitting with coffee cups at a table. Soap-opera-type music plays.*)

JANE: Lucy Dear, tell me, what's troubling you? You know I'm your best friend. You can tell me anything. Is it your husband? Did you kill someone? You know you can tell me, your best friend. You really shouldn't let little things get you down.

LUCY: No, no, it's nothing like that. I wouldn't be so upset, but I just can't cope. You see, I have . . .

(*Phone rings,* JANE *gets up to answer it.*)

JANE: Now, Lucy, just hold onto yourself. I'll be right back.

(JANE *goes offstage;* LUCY *finishes her coffee and puts the cup in her bag.* JANE *returns.*)

JANE: Now, Lucy, tell me your problem . . .

LUCY: Well, you see, I have this thing. I can't seem to, oh, it's too terrible to talk about! (*She begins to cry.*)

(*The doorbell rings, and* JANE *gets up to answer.*)

JANE: Lucy, take this tissue, and I'll be right back.

(*As* JANE *goes out the door,* LUCY *puts the entire box of tissues into her bag, thinks about it, then puts in the spoons, and finally takes* JANE'S *cup.*)

JANE (*as she returns*): Now, Lucy, that was just my mother. She's been hit by a car while crossing the street, but the ambulance took her away, so we can talk—now back to your problem.

LUCY: Oh, Jane, you're so good! What would I do without you?

JANE: That's what friends are for. Tell me your problem.

LUCY: Well, I have this compulsion; I can't control it. If you weren't such a good friend, I couldn't tell you. (*Now she is taking things openly, as if unable to stop.*) I steal, yeah, I take things. Oh, Jane, what will I do?

(JANE *takes out a whistle and blows it. Immediately, a* POLICE-MAN *appears and drags* LUCY *off.* LUCY *protests with tears and screams.* "*How could you—you're my friend!*" JANE *nonchalantly polishes her nails as* LUCY'S *cries fade. The end.*)

MC: Oh, that was so dramatic! Pull yourselves together, Ladies and Gentlemen, and we will hear another of the songs nominated for the worst song of the year. To present the song is "Davey Dog and the Bow-Wow-Wows." Give them a tremendous hand.

(DAVEY DOG AND THE BOW-WOW-WOWS *enter and sing badly.*)

MC: And now the awards you have been waiting for, special awards for very special people. (*This can be serious or funny. These awards should be for categories like the best sponsor, best play of the game, and the funniest goof. Use your imagination and then close the program effectively.*)

FRANK HART—POGO—SMITH is the author of this fun drama which originally appeared in his book, *52 Complete After-game Fellowships* (Nashville: Convention Press, 1980), p. 25. © Copyright 1980 ● The Sunday School Board of the Southern Baptist Convention. Used by permission.

As the Earth Rotates

This drama, patterned after the radio soap operas of decades ago, is adaptable for all types of occasions in churches and civic groups. It is especially helpful in preparation for an upcoming event like a sale for charity, a campaign in a church—you name it. Rewrite it as you please to fit your own occasion and situation.

CHARACTERS

ANNOUNCER:
NERVOUS NELLIE
MS. EM POSSIBLE
MR. PREP A. RATION

(*Do as a radio show with microphones and one person to sit at another mike and give signals . . . or set up the stage for a living room of days gone by—with furniture and other furnishings to look like the 1930s, 40s, or 50s. Fade in melodramatic music and begin to fade out as the* ANNOUNCER *speaks.*)

ANNOUNCER: And now another episode in the gripping drama, "As the Earth Rotates." Yesterday, when we left our heroine, Nervous Nellie, she was drained emotionally. Would she suffer a total nervous collapse? Would she be returned to the General Hospital? Would she be confined to recuperation for the duration? What strange fate awaits this bee-yeww-tee-full young ingenue? What new and exciting bee-yeww-tee-full people will step into her life? Time alone will tell. Let us gaze into her life as she ponders the perplexities of human existence.

(NELLIE *talks to herself.*)

NELLIE: Ohh, what shall I do? What shall I do? I have no place to turn. To work or not to work—that is the question, but what is the answer? That time of terror is looming around the corner. It's . . . it's . . . shudder . . . (*indicate the occasion*) time again!!! What shall I do? Yes, I know what I *ought* to do. But I simply cannot bring myself to it. Will I have the courage, the fortitude, to see it through? Last year (*or whenever the event last occurred*), perish the thought, I tried. Rahlly, I did (*sounding like Katharine Hepburn*). But after (*occasion*) I was confined to an institution. Who can I turn to—or is it whom? (*sobbing uncontrollably*)

(*knock at the door*)

NELLIE: (*answering the door*) Why, it's Ms. Em Possible. Do enter my humble domicile, Ms. Em. (*entering*)

MS. EM: Thank you, Sweetie. My, but you're not looking your usual self. Tsssk! Tsssk! Don't tell me that strange affliction is falling on you again. But I guess some people just can't get a firm grip on themselves.

NELLIE: Do sit down, Ms. Em. I'll pour us a cup of coffee (NELLIE *does*).

MS. EM: Why are you so worn out, Dearie? What kind of intrigue is going on?

NELLIE: Oh, darling Ms. Em, you're like a ray of light shining into the dark desolation of my little world (*aside: "Yeeccchhh!"*) Yes, there is something bothering me. But it's silly of me to mention it. No, I shan't. Rahlly, I shan't (*a la K. Hepburn again*).

Ms. Em: Yesss, do go on. After all, I may be able to throw even more light on the subject. You know, I recently finished a course on "How to Lose Friends and Alienate People." I'm humble about it, of course, but I consider myself quite an authority on life. Last year alone, with my assistance, three lovely homes were dashed to pieces. I consider myself an authority on life and love.

Nellie: There's no need to involve you, Ms. Em. No . . . no . . . but yes! I can't bear the pressure anymore. I must confide in you. This ordeal is— is —
more than I can bear alone. You see *(now shaking with weeping, wiping her eyes and nose with a hankie)*, oh, oh, boo hoo . . .

Mrs. Em: Yes, yes *(grinning sardonically)*, get on with it.

Announcer: We will return to "As the Earth Rotates" after this important message. Folks, are you tired, weak, run-down? Is life a drudge to you? Then maybe you haven't heard. Even your best friends may not tell you. Let us introduce you to an amazing product—it's new and improved. It's compact and small. It'll fit right into your pocket or purse. It will cure every ailment known to man and beast. It's guaranteed to outperform ointments, linaments, tonics, lotions, potions, pellets, pills, and powders. No person who is "in" can afford to be without one. If you are without one, hurry. Get one now. Come alive—and be in the peppy generation. *(Adapt the announcements and dialogue to fit the occasion.)* You didn't think you'd get by with only one commercial, did you? You are constantly cautioned about the seven danger signs. Here are those all-important signs if you are determined not to succeed:
1. lack of a definite date set up in the calendar, 2. failure to enlist enough workers *(or whatever)*, 3. ignorance of *(whatever*

again), 4. unwillingness to plan carefully now, 5. procrastination in *(whatever, ditto)*, 6. fostering a negative attitude about . . . , and 7. taking short cuts and cutting corners with . . .

The next part of our program is brought to you by . . . *(select what you want)*. Now we return to "As the Earth Rotates."

NELLIE: It's this thing I have about *(you choose)*. I just naturally dread it. Oh, the shame of it all!

MS. EM: Uh huh, exactly as I thought. My girl, why bother with it at all? It will only lead to a worsening of your condition. After all, a person in your condition doesn't need all that stress.

NELLIE: Oh, I've thought about that. But what about all the people depending on me(us)? Suppose others have this attitude. Shudder! You see, I'm in a quandary. I'm torn between two worlds!

MS. EM: Now, now, don't fret yourself. Your mascara is running. Besides, your copious tears will dilute the coffee.

NELLIE: *(biting her nails--she pretends to bite them)* The last time it was dreadfully tough, wasn't it? It was hot. It was cold. There were ups. There were downs. It wasn't a complete failure—but there was a certain shame to the matter. Sob! Sob! I wasn't personally prepared. Those who worked with me weren't prepared. Chaos was the result.

MS. EM: There, there, why not go ahead and give up? Throw in the towel. Back out. Bow out. Quit. Give in. Surrender. Finis. Kaput. Bail out. Resign. Go AWOL. Isn't it mahvel-ous how original I am? Surely you can do without all this anxiety. Think of old—er, young—number one.

NELLIE: But I can't have any peace. There is this unresolved conflict. Ms. Em, I have this sense of oughtness. The torture of non-participation becomes more severe than the struggles of last *(summer, fall, winter, spring, whatever)*.

MS. EM: Have I ever misled you?

NELLIE: Er—the fact is . . . *you have!*

MS. EM: Well, I never . . .

(Enter MR. PREP A. RATION. Dress him up like a fictional hero if you wish—a la Batman, Superman, Mighty Mouse, etc.)

MR. PREP: Mr. Prep is at your service. There's no reason to be nervous. When there is trouble and strife, I enter your life. Do not despair. Remember that I care.

NELLIE: Sigh, my knight in shining armor. Oh, excuse me I was carried away. But why are you here?

MR. PREP: I couldn't help hearing your anguish, your struggle with decision. I may have an answer that will lead to precision.

NELLIE: Oh, do not cease, Sir.

MR. PREP: You have explained the fears in your heart. I come to offer a proper start. Silk purses come not from sow's ears. Neither are problems solved with tears.

NELLIE: Yes, I finally understand. My tears have proved fruitless and vain!

MR. PREP: Preparation is the name of the game—and incidentally why I came.
After the date is set and people are on the line, I beg of you not to pine.

MS. EM: Your poetry grates on my nerves. Would you kindly speak in prose?

MR. PREP: Well, if you insist, I will desist. Ooopps, there I go again . . .

NELLIE: Yes, yes . . .

MS. EM: How dare you barge into here when I was solving all of Nellie's dilemmas?

NELLIE: Please allow this generous gentleman to continue. His words are balm to my grieved spirit.

MR. PREP: Thank you, gracious lady. First of all, may I be so bold as to ask: *(ask an important question relating to the event)?*

NELLIE: Well, kind Sir, partly.

MS. EM: Hmmppff—such as it is . . .

MR. PREP: And have you set the date, may I inquire?

NELLIE: Er, yes, but most of *(fill in)* felt that we ought to get by with as little as possible. If we don't ease up, we'll be left as empty shells of ourselves.

MS. EM: How true! I don't know why we fool with it, anyway.

MR. PREP: Allow me to counter those claims, ladies. Maybe some are empty shells because they were not properly prepared. Then, some may feel that this is not necessary, so they cop out by "getting by with as little as possible."

MS. EM: Well, what's wrong with that?

NELLIE: I will come to your defense, Mr. Prep. Everything you say is absolutely true. We are sorely guilty of going at this wrong.

MS. EM: I still insist I am correct, as usual.

MR. PREP: You see, ladies--attitude is half the battle. You will have as good a *(fill in the event)* as you desire. To quote an old phrase, "Where there's a will, there's a way."

NELLIE: Eureka! You're throwing more light on the subject.

Ms. Em: *(with irony in her tone)* Hmmppfff, it's just because I opened the blinds.

NELLIE: Please, my dear lady, stop your kidding. Please continue, Sir.

(At this point, promote various aspects of your event, singling out key factors you want the audience to recall. "Tailor-make" this part of the drama.)

PREP: Here I have the items that will sustain you, no matter the circumstances.

Ms. Em: That's patently ridiculous.

MR. PREP: Many will step forward to verify my claims.

NELLIE: I am enraptured, Prep. It all begins to gather in my innocent little mind. Oh joy! Oh goodie, goodie gum drop!

MR. PREP: Unlike Clerk Kant, ladies, I do not slip into a telephone booth. But there is this help in the *(program, materials, plans, etc.)*.

NELLIE: If only we had *(whatever)* last time out. Alas and alack, we were almost pulling hair before the *(event)* was over.

Ms. Em: *(with acid in her voice)* Well, lah-dee-dah!

MR. PREP: Miss Nellie, do you feel your work group did enough planning last time?

NELLIE: Well, Sir, we just decided we'd get together whenever we could--and believe me, Sir, that wasn't very much.

Ms. Em: Indeed, we have too many stupid meetings already.

MR. PREP: Ladies, it is trite but true: "Plan the work and work the plan."

NELLIE: Yes, yes, most battles are won the day before.

Ms. EM: *(sarcastically)* Wonderful! There's another original pearl of wisdom.

MR. PREP: The right kind of planning and preparation are keys that unlock the door to a successful *(event, whatever)*. Will you pledge, Miss Nellie, to follow these basic rudiments I have proposed.

NELLIE: Rudi--what?

Ms. EM: Basic fundamentals, little dummy!

MR. PREP: I mean, are you willing to try these simple suggestions?

NELLIE: Yes, oh yes, I have a high resolve. Already I feel a floodtide of calmness washing over me.

Ms. EM: *(Squeals in high-pitched voice)* Floodtide nothing! She put too much detergent in the washing machine!

ANNOUNCER: As the sun sinks in the West, as darkness enshrouds the earth, as stalwart Mr. Prep A. Ration departs the scene with a flourish, we leave Nellie who is no longer nervous. We bid a fond adieu as she and Ms. Em float from the house on a tidal wave of detergent foam.

This stirring saga has been brought to you by the makers of *(insert your own programs or products, etc.)*. Are you prepared for a successful *(whatever)?* You can be by latching onto *(you name it)*. You can learn valuable lessons from this slice of life.

Will Nellie persevere? Will she follow through on Mr. Prep's inspiration? Will she and her co-workers heed the Seven Danger Signs? Will they profit from the mistakes of the past? We have ample reasons to believe they will!

Original sayings of the week: An ounce of prevention is worth a pound of cure. It's not over until it's over— or until the fat lady (or man) sings. A bird in the hand is worth two in the bush. A stitch in time saves nine.

(Voice of Ms. Em *from offstage*: Those are so creative, aren't they?

This fun drama was contributed by Joseph S. Johnson, Jr., Broadman Products Department, The Baptist Sunday School Board, Nashville, Tennessee. Used by permission.

Murder on the American Express

CHARACTERS

MADAME JOSEPHINE LASUER: *wealthy French lady*
CROCKETT: MADAME LASUER'S *man servant*
MARY: MADAME LASUER'S *maid*
MORIARITY
WAITER
Famous Detectives:
    MICK and MOLLY CHARLES
    HERLOCK SHOLMES
    PIERRE HERCULES
    MRS. MARBLE
    RICKY DILLANE
    JESSICA KETCHER
    TERRY DAYSON

SETTING

The dining room of the cruise ship *The American Express*

PROPS

Several small tables (*such as game tables*) covered with table-cloths and set for a meal.
spooky music

SCENE 1

(*Scene opens in dining room of cruise ship. Room is empty.* MA-
DAME LaSUER *and her man servant* CROCKETT *enter.* WAITER
shows them to table, gives them a menu and leaves)

MADAME LaSUER: Ah, Crockett, at last we are here.

CROCKETT: Yes, Madame, finally, after so much planning.

MADAME: But how clever we are, Crockett. Have you seen all
the "participants"?

CROCKETT: Look, Madame, some are arriving now. Here is the
famous Mick and Molly Charles. They have solved many
murder cases . . . and put many criminals in jail!

MADAME (*gleefully*): Wonderful! Wonderful! Crockett, what
fun we are going to have!

(MICK *and* MOLLY *enter and are seated by waiter.*)

MICK: Well, we're here . . . although for the life of me I cannot
understand why.

MOLLY: Come on, Mick, where's your sense of adventure? We
get *real* cruise tickets through the mail for the fabulous
cruise ship, *The American Express.*

MICK: Well, Molly Dear, I only hope we aren't sorry we've
used them.

MOLLY: Oh, lighten up! What could happen?

(WAITER *enters again with two gentlemen,* HERLOCK SHOLMES
and RICKY DILLANE. SHOLMES *is costumed as* "Sherlock
Holmes," *and* DILLANE *as a typical tough* "Private Eye." *They
are seated at a table.*)

RICKY (*talks like tough guy*): So, Mr. Sholmes, you received a
ticket in the mail too. What kind of a caper is this?

SHOLMES: Elementary, my dear Dillane. Someone quite
wealthy—so wealthy that he or she could reserve this entire cruise ship for our party.

DILLANE: Oh yeah! Why, I'll get 'em.

SHOLMES: Calm down, old man. Logical reason and deduction will be our weapon.

(*Enter* MRS. MARBLE *and* JESSICA KETCHER. WAITER *seats* MRS. MARBLE *at table with the* CHARLESES *and* JESSICA *at table with* SHOLMES *and* DILLANE.)

MICK: Let me introduce myself and my wife . . .

MRS. MARBLE (*interrupting*): Oh, I know you are those famous detectives, Mick and Molly Charles.

MOLLY: Oh my, I read all of the Mrs. Marble stories!

MICK: Why were we sent free ticket to this cruise?

MOLLY: Did you get a ticket in the mail too, Mrs. Marble?

MRS. MARBLE: Why, yes, dear, you did too?

(*Men at other table stand as* JESSICA *is seated.* RICKY *tips his hat.*)

SHOLMES: Mrs. Ketcher, we are honored to have you join our little group.

DILLANE: How'd you know the dame's name, Sholmes?

SHOLMES: Dillane, old man, you surely must recognize Jessica Ketcher, famous writer of murder mysteries?

DILLANE (*to* JESSICA): Did you get a free ticket, too?
JESSICA: Why yes, I did, Mr. . . .?

DILLANE: Dillane, famous private eye.

JESSICA: What do you make of all this?

(WAITER *brings in and seats* PIERRE HERCULES *and* TERRY DAYSON. PIERRE *is very French, with accent.* TERRY *is large, dressed in suit, tie, etc.*)

PIERRE: Ah, Mr. Dayson, look around you. What do you see?

TERRY: There's Jessica Ketcher, Rick Dillane, Mrs. Marble, Mick and Molly Charles, and Herlock Sholmes. Many

crooks would like to do away with the people in this room.
What do you make of this, Pierre?

PIERRE: We are all gathered here aboard *The American Express*
for a most mysterious and nefarious purpose. Before this is
over, I will be called on to use my little grey cells.

(*Blackout*)

SCENE 2

(*The next evening. The room is cleared of tables. Chairs are
pushed back and placed in groups, to allow as much room as
possible for movement. All characters except* MADAME LASUER,
CROCKETT, MARY, WAITER, *and* MORIARITY *enter and stand
or sit in small groups, talking.*)

MARY (*the maid runs in screaming*): Someone come quickly!
Madame LaSuer has been stabbed, poisoned, and shot!

CROCKETT (*coming in behind* MARY): Yes, Madame is dead,
how frightful! Murdered in her bed in her locked cabin.
(*All detectives come and stand around* CROCKETT.) I'm
glad you are all here! You must find the murderer right
away . . . We dock in two hours. Catch him before he can
get off the ship!

(*All freeze. Boat whistle blows, and lights go out. Scary music
begins in background. All characters move around as if search-
ing for clues . . . some have flashlights they turn off and on. Some
have candles.* DILLANE *has cigarette lighter he turns off and on.*
SHOLMES, *of course, has a huge magnifying glass. They move
around, bumping into each other, etc. This can be kept up as long
as it is funny.*)

SCENE 3

(*One hour later. All the characters enter. They stand or sit in
small groups. They look suspiciously at each other. In the group
now are* CROCKETT, *the* WAITER, *and the maid,* MARY. *In the*

center of the room is a large arm chair, covered with an afghan or blanket.)

CROCKETT: Who shall begin to solve this tragic murder? Mr. Sholmes, as our senior member, would you take charge of the proceedings?

SHOLMES (*coming forward*): I believe it's customary to start with the ladies: Shall we begin with Mrs. Marble?

MRS. MARBLE: Thank you, Mr. Sholmes. We shall get this over with quickly! There can be only one conclusion since no one could have left the ship. It must be one of us in this room. (*All characters react.*) We were allowed to examine the body separately. I discovered a wound, a small-caliber pistol wound. Since Mrs. Jessica Ketcher is the only one who carries a pistol of this caliber, I came to this conclusion! Mrs. Ketcher is the long-lost niece of Madame La-Suer and will inherit her millions. She took this opportunity to murder Madame LaSuer for her money, which she will inherit.

SHOLMES: What detective work, Mrs. Marble! Bravo! Do we all agree with her solution?

JESSICA: I certainly do not! I am Madame LaSuer's niece, but I did not kill her!

MICK and MOLLY (*together*): Of course not!

MICK: Jessica was with us playing cards when the murder took place.

SHOLMES: Do you two have a solution, then?

MOLLY: Yes, at least I think so, don't we, Mick?

MICK: You bet, Honey! It happened this way . . . while we were playing cards, I saw Mr. Dillane go past our cabin. He looked suspicious, so I followed him. He went to Madame LaSuer's cabin, and, oh, by the way, Madame was poisoned!

ALL but SHOLMES: Poisoned? Impossible, that's not what I saw . . .

MICK: Yes, I found an empty bottle of sleeping pills by her bed. Someone put the pills into her coffee . . . and who could do that? Dillane, her lost grandson! He's the one who will get her millions!

DILLANE: Wait a minute! You can't pin that rap on me! I went to see the old dame, but I didn't kill her! She was stabbed— not poisoned, anyway.

(All react with shock, etc.)

SHOLMES: Then, Mr. Dillane, you tell us who stabbed Madame LaSuer!

DILLANE: Why, Crockett, of course. He's really her dead husband's business partner. He was cheated out of his part of the business, and now he's getting his revenge! Simple, huh?

CROCKETT: Nonsense! Madame and I were close friends as well as employer and employee. You are way off! Mary and I were strolling on the deck at the time of Madame's murder.

DILLANE: Oh, yeah! Likely story, there's always a dame involved in these cases. (*To* MARY) You helped him, didn't you? (MARY *begins to cry.*)

SHOLMES: Before we call the police . . . let's hear from one of our other distinguished detectives. Mrs. Ketcher . . .

JESSICA: Well, I certainly did not kill my dear auntie . . . Mrs. Marble is obviously getting senile! I can tell you who is the murderer . . . It's Terry Dayson!

(MR. DAYSON *rises partly from his chair . . . although he can hardly get out of it!*)

TERRY: And what evidence do you have to support that accusation, my dear?

JESSICA: I know you lost a case that Madama LaSuer brought against a client of yours . . . and you've never forgiven her. You've lost only one case in your whole life! She was the only one who could claim beating the famous lawyer, Terry Dayson!

DAYSON (*shaken*): You still haven't proven your case.

JESSICA: How's this? I couldn't sleep last night. Just as I started up to the deck to get some fresh air, I saw you coming out of Madame's room. I could hardly miss seeing you. I followed you to the deck, and you threw something overboard. . . . Was it a knife, Mr. Dayson?

TERRY: You'll never know! Your evidence is just circumstantial. Yes, I went to see Madame LaSuer. We had some business to discuss. I'm to be executer of her will. We signed all the papers. It was just business! (*He begins to get upset.*) And I should have won that case . . . *the judge was biased . . . the witnesses lied . . .*

SHOLMES: Get control of yourself, old Boy . . . Do you know who the murderer is?

TERRY: Yes . . . I do! By all means, I'll tell you! Mick Charles planned all this. It's been so long since he and Molly have had a good case to solve . . . he planned to get us all here and then kill Madame in order to claim to find her killer. Just admit it, Charles!

MICK: Surely that's the most nonsensical solution of all these nonsensical solutions. My deductions are right! Molly and I always solve our cases!

(*All begin to move around, accusing each other, talking, shouting.*)

SHOLMES: Silence! Ladies and gentlemen! Silence!

PIERRE (*has been rather quiet during all this exchange . . . looking wise, as if observing all the people.*): Ah, yes, Sholmes,

thank you for getting the quietness. Now, me, I, the greatest detective alive, may speak. All are protesting too much!
There's only one answer: a conspiracy! Crockett and Mary
sent the invitations, telling Madame that they were planning a gala for her. All of you that were invited took the
opportunity to confuse the issue by stabbing, poisoning,
and shooting her. Thus no one was responsible, but *all*
killed her!

(*All react with shock, outrage, etc.*)

SHOLMES: Enough! This has gone on long enough! All of you be
quiet! And again I say: Silence!

(*Some sit down, others remain standing.*)

SHOLMES: This is a farce! Don't any of you realize how elementary this is? (*He walks to armchair that is stage center and
dramatically whips blanket from chair. In the chair is the
evil-looking* MORIARITY.)

(*All mumble in shock and unbelief*)

SHOLMES: Good evening, Moriarity! (*To others*) You see before
you the evil genius, Moriarity. Moriarity has been my
nemesis for years. It was his evil design to dress as Madame LaSuer and fake "her" death, hoping he could dis-
credit all of us! (*Turns suddenly*) Dillane, watch Crockett
and the maid, Mary. Hold all of them for the police—they
had to be in on the scheme. The police will see if the real
Madame LaSuer is alive and well! Until then we must de-
tain these scoundrels! Take them away . . .

(*As Dillane proceeds to take* CROCKETT *and* MARY *prisoners,*
TERRY DAYSON *manages to get close to* MORIARITY)

TERRY: Mr. Moriarity, could you use a good lawyer?

(*Blackout*)

II.

FUN DRAMAS SHORTER IN LENGTH

Star Journey

This epic asks the question: "Who's Ugly?" It is a takeoff on "Star Trek." It should be done with the following characters.

CHARACTERS

CAPTAIN BURT who reads the CAPTAIN'S LOG
LT. SPECK
ENGINEER DOTTY
THE GRAND GROMET
DR. ROMAL
DR. MOLERK VOICE
Several people who wear sacks on their heads
   (*Production note: each time the captain's log is read, the room is blacked out, with only the voice of the* CAPTAIN *heard.*)

PROPS

as much gadgetry as possible: flashing lights, weird costumes and hairdos, all the fake electronic equipment that can be obtained
dry ice
paper sacks
Halloween mask

CAPTAIN'S LOG: Star date three krognigs and two weegils into
   the month of Rancil. We had completed our assignment of
   investigating the Woolsigs on the newfound asteroid of

Plankton when the trouble began. First, the engines began to run badly. We couldn't get a warp three without engine ping! Dotty, our engineer, finally put in some new spark plugs, and that helped take care of part of the trouble. But we still had limited power. Do you know how much spark plugs cost for a star ship? Ridiculous! But Dotty is a fine engineer, and she managed. I think she used a hair pin, which is remarkable since she is utterly bald.

Next, the guards found a stowaway on board who could melt the metal on the food bins. We caught him just in time. He had eaten almost all the food. And since we could not throw him out into space, he too was destined for Maythall. Now, Maythall is not my favorite place. The people are so ugly, they wear sacks on their heads, so they won't have to look at each other. Our mission, to take two plastic surgeons to Maythall to see if they could help those poor people.

CAPTAIN (*to* LT. SPECK): Well, Speck, are we on course for Maythall?

SPECK: Yes, Captain, but there's something peculiar out there.

CAPTAIN: Peculiar? What do you mean peculiar?

SPECK: Captain, it's getting bigger, it's like a . . . a fog. It will swallow the ship in exactly two sonnets and one pulse.

CAPTAIN: Well, Speck, what shall we do?

SPECK: Captain, I can't presume to tell our esteemed captain what to do. You speak, I follow. (*Over intercom*) Dotty, Dotty, give us warp speed ten. Get us out of here.

DOTTY (*voice over intercom*): Sorry, Captain, I'll have to have some lanobine before I can get warp ten out of these engines.

CAPTAIN: Well, where can we get some lanobine?

DOTTY: Where we are headed: Maythall.

CAPTAIN: Well, give me all the speed you can.

DOTTY: Aye, Aye, Captain!

SPECK: Maybe we can outrun it, Captain!

CAPTAIN: No, Speck, turn on the microscreen. (*Speaking to the screen*) Now, whoever—whatever you are out there—this is Captain Burt of the *Star Ship Centerprize.* What do you want?

VOICE: I want your ship.

CAPTAIN: You cannot have my ship, and you are in my way. I must get to Maythall on an important mission. I must help those desperately ugly people!

VOICE: Sorry, Captain, I need your ship.

CAPTAIN: Why do you need my ship?

VOICE: It's cold out here, and I need a ride.

CAPTAIN: Well, come on board. You'll have to go to Maythall with the rest of the uglies. That's the best we can do.

VOICE: OK, Captain, I'll ooze on board. (*Comes on board as fog: container of dry ice is pushed on stage.*)

CAPTAIN: You are welcome. Just stay out of my way until we get to Maythall.

FOG: Certainly, Captain!

(*The container that holds the dry ice is taken off stage.*)

CAPTAIN: I can't believe this, Speck. How did we get all these weirdos on board the *Star Ship Centerprize*? Hope they don't contaminate it!

SPECK: Now, Captain, you know it's part of our mission to protect all life in space.

CAPTAIN: Yes, Speck, but don't push it. You're kind of weird yourself.

DOTTY (*voice on intercom*): Captain, Captain!

CAPTAIN: Yes, Dotty?

DOTTY: We can get warp speed six now.

CAPTAIN: Good, Dotty, let's get this over with!

CAPTAIN'S LOG: 0600 hours. We are nearing Maythall. I must get myself in hand. I don't know when I've dreaded an assignment as much. I certainly hope everyone will keep the sacks on their heads, and I won't have to look at those ugly people. It's very hard when one is so handsome. Others are not so fortunate to be one of the beautiful people. But I will be strong and carry out this task with my usual efficiency.

SPECK (*interrupting*): Captain, we are approaching Maythall. Are you ready to transport?

CAPTAIN: Yes, Speck, as ready as I will ever be. See to a party of engineers to locate the lanobine. Get the Fog and that—whatever it is—and transport them first. You and I and Dotty will accompany the doctors and meet the rulers of Maythall. I'll meet you in the transporter room.

SPECK: Captain, perhaps if you would wear a sack on your head, it would make the people more comfortable, and you would not be so noticeable when you get nauseated.

CAPTAIN: Good idea, Speck. But what about you?

SPECK: I never get nauseated. That's a feeling.

CAPTAIN: Oh, yes, I forgot. Let's go! (*He places sack on his head.*)

CAPTAIN'S LOG: 0700 hours. We transported to Maythall and

were greeted by a group of people wearing sacks on their heads. I took charge.

CAPTAIN: Whom do I have the pleasure of addressing?

GRAND GROMET: I am the Grand Gromet of Maythall. We greet you. Who are you?

CAPTAIN: I am Captain Burt of the *Star Ship Centerprize.* We have been sent here to help you underprivileged, ugly people. This is my second in command, Lt. Speck; our engineer, Dotty; and Drs. Romal and Dr. Molerk, who will perform the necessary procedures to cure your ugliness.

GRAND GROMET: You are welcome! The people of Maythall welcome you!

CAPTAIN: Thank you, and now the doctors will get to work while we begin our search for lanobine. Lead the way, Dotty.

CAPTAIN'S LOG: We began our search for lanobine immediately. I hoped we would meet no one without a sack on the head. Lt. Speck, Dotty, and the engineering crew soon found the lanobine. The crew was transported back to the ship to begin the needed repairs on the engine. We went in search of the doctors.

CAPTAIN (*pointing at the audience*): Speck, do you believe your eyes? Look at that beautiful girl! The doctors must have been successful!

SPECK: It appears so, Captain. Shall we find the good doctors?

CAPTAIN: Yes, indeed, they are to be congratulated. Ah, here they come now! What a miracle you have performed! And, Grand Gromet, how handsome you are!

GRAND GROMET: Yes, it is a miracle! Now, Captain, you can remove your head sack so we may all gaze on one another in friendship.

CAPTAIN: Of course, Grand Gromet. (*He removes his sack. He is grotesquely ugly. He has put on a Halloween mask during the* CAPTAIN'S LOG—*blackout.*)

SPECK: Oh, Captain, excuse me . . . I'm nauseated!

GRAND GROMET: I'm sorry, Captain, I must leave the sight of you . . . you are . . . ugly!

CAPTAIN: Me, ugly? No, that's not possible.

DR. MOLERK: Captain, we forgot to tell you, it's the lanobine that makes one ugly. But don't worry, we'll go back to the ship for some antidote. (*He leads the* CAPTAIN *off, saying, "There, there, it's all right," etc., while the* CAPTAIN *sobs uncontrollably.*)

Happy Birthday, America!

Originally written for the Bicentennial celebration, this fun drama could be used on many patriotic occasions, especially Fourth of July celebrations or banquets.

CHARACTERS

MASTER OF CEREMONIES   JOHN HANCOCK
GEORGE WASHINGTON   MESSENGER BOY
BEN FRANKLIN   FRANCIS SCOTT KEY
PAUL REVERE   WAITRESS
MRS. PAUL REVERE   SINGER
(*Costumes should be recognizable close to the period and character.*)

SCENE 1

PROPS

Poor Richard's Almanac
tape recording of rain and thunder
large key on a string
a miner's hat or tape a small flashlight to BEN FRANKLIN'S hat

MC: Ladies and Gentlemen, I'm happy to welcome you to a

birthday party for our nation: the United States of America! We spent months researching the material for this program we are presenting, and we hope you will appreciate a new look at the history of our country. And now for the first time, it can be told! This is the way it really happened. First of all, we will hear from the most famous man of our country's history: President George Washington!

GEORGE WASHINGTON (*at the microphone*): Gentlemen, when in the course of human events . . . one is asked to be president of a new nation, one must ask some questions:
1. How much is the salary?
2. When can Martha and I move into the White House?
3. What is the oval office?
4. Do I have to have Henry Kissinger in my cabinet? (*These questions should be updated with current events.*)

MC: Thank you, Mr. President. I'm sure all of your questions will be answered. (GEORGE *exits.*) To continue our salute to our nation, we will sing, "You're a Grand Old Flag."

SCENE 2

(BEN FRANKLIN *enters on end of song. As song ends there is a violent clap of thunder. He shakes the rain off his coat.*)

BEN FRANKLIN: Friends, I'm Benjamin Franklin, and I have come here to talk with you about my inventions. There's the Franklin stove, very economical, saves valuable fuel. I've also invented the lighting rod; you'll understand why it's needed in a few moments. And then, there's my book, *Poor Richard's Almanac.* With your indulgence, I will read a few bits of wisdom from its pages. (*While he reads a few selected passages, the storm gets worse.* BEN *inspects a large key on a string. As he is holding the string,* BEN *turns and* speaks.) I am about to discover electricity. You will be here to see it. When the lightning is just right, this key will light up, and I will have discovered electricity.

(*About this time* BEN'S *hat lights up, and he runs from the room. Flashing the lights off and on would also be a good effect. Have the music "Yankee Doodle Dandy" begin as soon as Ben is off stage. This could be a group song or solo.*)

SCENE 3

(PAUL REVERE *enters with his shoes in his hand, trying to sneak out the door. Suddenly,* MRS. PAUL REVERE *enters.*)

MRS. REVERE: Paul Revere! Where do you think you're going?

PAUL: I've got to warn the town that the British are coming, Dear.

MRS. REVERE: That's terrible! That's the worse excuse I've ever heard for getting out of the house. Just how do you plan to tell everyone in Boston that the British are coming?

PAUL: Well, you see, Angel, I'm going to ride through the town, pound on the doors, and yell, "*The British are coming!*"

MRS. REVERE: You no-good scroundrel! Just how do you know the British are coming?

PAUL: Well, you see, Sweetie, there's a lantern in the belfry of the church. One, if by land, and two, if by sea . . . or is it two, if by land, and one, if by sea?

MRS. REVERE: It's just getting worse and worse . . . what a ridiculous story! If you want to go out that bad, go on! The British are coming, indeed! (she exits.) (PAUL *puts on his shoes and goes toward door. He stops and looks at the audience.*)

PAUL: Don't laugh . . . it got me out of the house, didn't it?

(*Music: Group singing: "America the Beautiful"*)

SCENE 4

(JOHN HANCOCK *sits at a desk writing. There is a large stack of paper on the desk. He writes one large letter [as A,B,C, etc.] at a time on each page and drops it in a box by the desk.*)

JOHN HANCOCK: Boy!

(MESSENGER BOY *enters.*)

JOHN: Deliver this letter to the Continental Congress.

BOY (*as he picks up heavy box and staggers to the door with it*): Gee, Mr. Hancock, why can't you write small like everyone else?

(*Music: Group singing: "America"*)

SCENE 5

(*There is the noise of battle in the background.* FRANCIS SCOTT KEY *is seated at a table agitatedly trying to write something on a piece of paper.*)

FRANCIS SCOTT KEY (*gets up and shouts*): Stop that noise! How can I think? How can I compose? Stop it, I say! (*The noise stops.*) Ah, that's better . . . now . . . (*He hums "The Blue Danube Waltz" or any other nonrelated musical number.*) Somehow I don't think they'll sing that at football games, I'd better try something else. (*Have someone sing "The Star Spangled Banner" as* FRANCIS *continues to think. He jumps up, looks out the window, as if at the battle.*) That's it! That's it! Perfect! (*He runs off as the group picks up melody and sings along with the soloist.*)

(PATRICK HENRY *enters and sits at a table.* WAITRESS *approaches table.*)

WAITRESS: What can I give you, Sir?

PATRICK: What can you give me? (*stands*) My friends, I will have freedom! The greatest thing in the world is freedom! Without freedom I cannot exist. There is nothing in life without freedom! Nothing! (*He shouts*) *Give me liberty or give me death!*

WAITRESS: Will you have it here or to go?

(*Music: "God Bless America"*)
Close the evening with a talk entitled: "What America means to me."

Show and Tell

CHARACTERS

TEACHER	ABBIE
RENEE	ROBIN
MELTON	SANDY
JEFF	AMY
SHAUNA	JAMEY
ALLISON	

All characters act as preschool children except the teacher. They speak in in childish voices. Create the atmosphere of a preschool room. The children will wiggle, push each other, talk, and express excitement about Show and Tell Day. Seat the children on the floor or in low chairs facing the teacher. Some of the children will have their backs or sides to the audience. The animals are imaginary. Each person must make the audience "see" his/her pet, how big, how small, what color, and how the pet moves, etc.

TEACHER: One of the most exciting days at our school is "Show and Tell" Day. This week we have asked each pupil to bring their favorite pet to show to our class. All right, children, if you will get quiet, we'll begin. Who wants to be first? (*All children raise their hands, wave them.*) Robin, we'll start with you. Come up to the front and show us what you've brought and tell us about it.

ROBIN (*Holds arms as if she has rabbit. Strokes it.*): I have a pet rabbit. His name is Peter. He is a white rabbit with pink ears. I feed him grass and rabbit pellets. I love my rabbit.

TEACHER: Thank you, Robin. What a nice pet. You may put him back in his hutch now. (*Pause while* ROBIN *does as told.*) Who will be next? How about you, Sandy, what did you bring?

SANDY: I brought a turtle. He is a box turtle. This is a poem about a turtle. "I had a little turtle, and his name was Joe. I wanted him to go fast, but he went slow."

TEACHER: How nice, Sandy! You may be seated now. (*The other children look at the turtle in its box. Poke at it, etc.*) Well, let's go on. Amy and Jamey, our twins, will be next. What did you two bring?

AMY: I don't have a pet.

JAMEY: Yes, you do!

AMY: You always had a pet. I didn't have a pet! (*She's getting upset.*)

JAMEY: Yes, you did!

AMY: You can't call a *chicken* a pet!

JAMEY: Well, he followed you everywhere!

AMY: But you had a dog! (*By this time she is very upset. She begins pushing Jamey.*) Mom and Dad got you a dog!

JAMEY: Well, yeah . . .

AMY (*Now at the point of tears*): Your dog ate my chicken!

TEACHER: Now, children . . . you mustn't fight . . . Amy, maybe you can have a dog later. Let's go on to Renee . . .

RENEE: I brought my hamster. He runs around in a little wheel (*turns to teacher*). Why doesn't he get dizzy?

JEFF (*From the back of the room*): Because he's so dumb!

TEACHER: Jeff, that's enough! Go on, Renee.

RENEE: His name is Fur Ball. One day he got out of the cage, and Mommy wouldn't come home until Daddy caught him.

JEFF: Hamsters are dumb!

TEACHER: Jeff, come up here and sit by me if you can't keep quiet. (*He does, but makes faces, talks when teacher has her head turned. Children wave their hands, wanting to be next.*) Allison, you may be next.

ALLISON: Just a minute. (*She goes stage right and comes back with her monkey, imaginary, of course.*) This is a monkey. His name is George. He climbs the curtains. We laugh at George. He swings from the lights. Mommy makes me keep him in a cage . . . I don't know why.

JEFF: Because he's so dumb!

TEACHER: Jeff! Do you want to be sent from the room?

JEFF: No . . . I haven't shown my pet, yet.

TEACHER: If you want to show your pet you'd better behave. (*She is beginning to get a bit harried.*) Abbie, you come and show your pet.

ABBIE (*Holding out index finger*): This is Roscoe. Roscoe is a blue and green parakeet. He is sometimes a bad boy and says naughty words. (*To Roscoe*) Don't say nothin', Roscoe. Roscoe can whistle, flap his wings, eat, drink, and dirty in the bottom of his cage. (*While the other children say "oooh" she looks pleased and continues to hold Roscoe.*)

TEACHER: All right, Abbie, please place Roscoe back in his cage. Thank you, Dear. And now, Melton, it's your turn.

MELTON (*He has a big dog.*): This is my dog Susie. Susie is a Saint Bernard. She likes to lick you in the face. When she stands on her hind legs, she can steal the roast right off the table, like she did last night. Mama got real mad! Daddy says to ask if anyone wants to take Susie home for a pet.

JEFF: I do! I do!

AMY: No, I want Susie; I don't have a pet.

TEACHER (*Shouting*): Children! Children! You must settle down! (*They become quiet.*) Now, that's better. Thank you, Melton . . . she's really *big*! Tie her leash there in the back of the room. (*Melton drags Susie and ties her to a chair.*) We have time for just a few more. Jeff, you can be next.

JEFF (*goes to a box, takes out an incredibly long snake. It curls around his body. The children squeal.*): This is Josephine. She is a South American python. She can squeeze a person to death, but she loves me, and she won't hurt me. (*He addresses someone in the audience.*) So, Butch, you'd better stop pickin' on me, or I'm gonna sic my snake on you!

TEACHER (*quickly losing control of the situation*): Please, Jeff, put Josephine back in the box. I'm sure she is a very nice snake. (*Frantically*) Who's next? Oh yes, Shauna. What pet have you brought to show to us today? A kitty? Thank goodness!

SHAUNA: This is my kitty Precious. Isn't she pretty? I love my kitty. She sleeps with me at night. Precious eats cat food, milk, mice, and birds. (*About this time* ABBIE'S *Roscoe gets loose, Precious stalks Roscoe,* SHAUNA *stalks Precious. By this time all the animals* AND *the children are getting into the act. Susie is dragging the chair she's tied to trying to chase Precious. The children are running around or climbing on chairs, etc., trying to catch Roscoe. Finally, Roscoe is back in his cage, and Precious is back in her box. Everyone settles down.*)

TEACHER (*Disheveled and wiping brow*): Children, thank you

for bringing your pets. I'm sure that I'm going to be sick tomorrow. Those of you who did not get to show a pet may bring your pet to show tomorrow to Mrs. Jones, my substitute. You may go now. (*She falls into a chair, totally exhausted.*)

Katts

CHARACTERS

MASTER OF CEREMONIES
LOTUS FLOWER: *Siamese.*
TUFFY: *Katt-around-town. He's seen a lot of living; perhaps one ear would be rather beaten up.*
PYEWACKET: *Very sophisticated katt of soft color*
MARFIELD: *Yellow and large*
PROFESSOR JOHNSON

COSTUMES

Dress all katts in loose-fitting costumes, to resemble katts (katts) as closely as possible. Use eye makeup for outlining slanted eyes and colors suitable for character. Add ears and whiskers for total effect. The PROFESSOR should have glasses, rumpled suit, string tie: typical absentminded professor.

MC: Welcome, my friends, to another of our informative series: "eye makeup for outlining
slanted eyes and colors suitable for character. Add ears and whiskers for total effect. The PROFESSOR should have glasses, rumpled suit, string tie: typical absentminded professor.

MC: Welcome, my friends, to another of our informative series: "Thirty Minutes." (We don't have enough time for "Sixty Minutes.") Tonight our topic is "Katts." Not since the days of Cleopatra have katts been in such popularity. We see them as cartoon characters and in comic strips, movies, TV, and commercials. They are on T-shirts, dishes, pajamas, and shoes . . . katts are everywhere. I was wondering the other day what katts think of all this popularity. Well, why not ask them? We have with us tonight several distinguished katts. We'll ask each one to tell us about themselves and how they are reacting to the spotlight. First, the extremely beautiful Lotus Flower.

LOTUS FLOWER (Oriental accent): Oh, you are so good to ask beautiful Lotus Flower to express humble opinion. I believe felines are the most graceful and beautiful of all creatures, so why should we not be honored as is our due? As I was telling my master the other evening, just as he put me out, it's unthinkable for me to be out in the cold. But he seemed to resent my using his angora sweater for a scratching mat. Ah, humans are so mysterious and hard to understand.

(*She takes a seat behind the* MC, *as all* katts *do when they finish.*)

MC: Thank you, Lotus Flower, I can't imagine anyone putting you outside. Now let's hear from Tuffy, Katt-About-Town.

TUFFY (Swaggers in, speaks with a gangster-type accent): Boy, is that one a gorgeous doll! (*He goes over to* LOTUS *but* MC *brings him back.*) Well, what I say is, it's about time us katts got our just dues! We've been keeping rats and mice outta houses and barns for centuries. And look at de tanks we get! Kicked from place to place. But, man, we're survivors! So tell me how great I am—I love it!

MC: Has your life changed since this trend of the popularity of katts?

TUFFY: Oh, like *wow*! Has it? I eat regular like now. Even have a little catnip on the side once-in-a-while. And laps . . . laps are great! So soft and warm!

MC: Thank you, Tuffy . . . hope all nine of your lives are happy ones. Our next guest is Miss Pyewacket. She has a most interesting story to tell.

PYE: I was an abandoned cat. At least that's what my people think. Before now I was working for people who gave me very little respect. My previous owners abused animals for their bidding. They used animals to do their bidding and run their errands and such. Well, I got tired of doing all that running around for ungrateful weirdos. So I just caused myself to appear on Main Street one day. That's where my man person found me, and I let him take me home with him. I seldom have to use my wiles anymore, except to get more milk or to get left inside or to get more petting. You see we katts are of the nobility, and we are finally getting our deserved attention. But then, I always have.

MC: What more can I say? Do we have katts, or do they have us? Let's have the most famous cat of all answer these questions. Let's welcome Marfield!

MARFIELD: What a foolish question! Without a doubt people control katts! Our people feed us, pet us, and give us a place to live. And we katts give back so much to people. Such as, we chase mice (sometimes). Uh, we, uh, (*as if thinking*), uh, yes, keep their laps warm, uh, and feet warm as we sleep on the bottom of the bed. Of course, we katts are controlled by people, what else? (*He smiles and winks at other* katts.)

MC: Why did I ever doubt? And now to close. It is our distinct pleasure to have Professor Johnson from State University, an expert on the subject of "Kattatology." Welcome, Professor. Professor, what do you think has caused the rise in the popularity of katts?

PROFESSOR (*carries a cat*): You have come to the right person. I know everything you ever wanted to know about katts. I mean everything! Ask me something.

MC: I just did, Professor. I asked you why katts are so popular as pets today?

PROFESSOR: Why, dear man, because they are so easily trained and obedient. They are docile, never harming one's person or household goods.

MC: Well, you are the expert, but let's ask our katt panel? Is this true, panel?

(*The panel of* katts *roll their eyes skyward, place their paws in a prayer position, and meow for the* PROFESSOR.)

PROFESSOR: See, They are not exceptionally bright.

MC: Professor, what else can you tell us about katts in today's society?

PROFESSOR: Katts are very easy to get along with. Always predictable. They exist only to fulfill their master's wishes. Katts eat what is put before them. (*In the background the cat panel is beginning to break into cat laughter.*) Never finicky. Because of this, katts are not expensive to keep. They eat whatever is left over. (Katts *are now doubled over with laughter. They come and get the* PROFESSOR, *patting him on the back and putting arms around him, they take him off stage.*)

MC (*After the panel and the* PROFESSOR *have gone*): I'm glad we were able to explode all the myths surrounding katts and their lives. They are just simple, uncomplicated, loving creatures. (*Looks at watch.*) Oh my, I must hurry. My katt has to be fed at (*present time*) every day, and I'm out of that special food she likes. (*mumbling*) Oh, I'll never make it on time . . . I must hurry, etc. (*hurries off.*)

The Scary Movie

CHARACTERS

RACHEL: *Has been married several years and is not excited about an evening at the movies with her husband*

JERRY: *Has persuaded his wife, RACHEL, to accompany him to the movies*

IRVING: *Young man*

BETSY: *Young woman (preferable for actors playing IRVING and BETSY either to be married or going steady in real life)*

DENNIS: *Grade school boy*

BRENT: *Grade school boy*

SARAH LOU: *Extremely overweight woman*

VOICE: *Dramatic reader offstage*

POLICEMAN: *reader offstage*

THE SQUASH: *An ugly yellow "thing"*

SETTING

The setting is a movie theater. The set is empty when the skit begins, and as in a real theater, the patrons begin to file in by twos or singly. First to arrive is a couple that has been married several years. Movies are now strictly for entertainment, not for holding hands. He has persuaded her to see "The Return of the Killer Squash" much against her will.

The next couple to arrive is obviously madly in love. The couple can see nothing but each other.

Next are two grade-school boys who sneaked off to see the movie. Mom and Dad had warned they would have nightmares if they saw it.

Attending by herself is an extremely overweight lady. She is loaded down with popcorn, cold drinks, and candy bars. Her motive for attending the movie is readily seen.

The lights are still on as the action starts. As the movie begins the lights are dimmed. Use a soft spot on the actors or a projector light. Experiment to get just the right effect.

PROPS

seven chairs in a row to simulate the rows at the movie.
recorded music
Costume for SQUASH is a loose, yellow garment. Over the head use a sack painted yellow. Cut out eye holes, of course.

(JERRY *and* RACHEL *enter.*)

RACHEL: Jerry, you know I didn't want to come to this movie. Why did you insist?

JERRY: I just thought it might be exciting. Remember when we used to go to the movies every Saturday night, regardless of what was on? We didn't see the movie anyway. (*He tries to take her hand.*)

RACHEL (*Pulling her hand away*): Jerry, you stop that! You'd think we were terrible when we were dating!

(*They settle in their seats.*)

JERRY: Well, you just imagine you're in the movies when we were dating about ten years ago. Bet you'll remember. (*He puts his arm around her; she puts it down.*)

(*About this time,* IRVING *and* BETSY *enter. They push past* JERRY *and* RACHEL *and sit, leaving one seat between the couples.* IRVING *is very solicitous of* BETSY. *He helps her as she sits.*

He asks her if she is comfortable, if the seats are right, etc. BETSY *giggles a lot.)*

JERRY (*Whispering to* RACHEL): See Rachel, that's how we used to act.

RACHEL (*Leaning over to look*): I certainly hope not!

(DENNIS *and* BRENT *enter. They swagger in, trying to look as if they had permission to see this scary movie. They push past* RACHEL *and* JERRY, *past* BETSY *and* IRVING, *and sit on the other side of them. They are carrying popcorn and cold drinks. They snicker and push each other, and* DENNIS *spills his drink on* BETSY. *She jumps up and brushes herself.* RACHEL *and* JERRY *look on, shaking their heads at the kids of today.* IRVING *tells the boys to be more careful, and he and* BETSY *go back to their own world, gazing at each other and whispering in each other's ears, even sneaking a kiss now and then. This sets the boys off, and* DENNIS *and* BRENT *begin to pantomime* BETSY *and* IRVING.)*

RACHEL: What time is it, Jerry? Is this movie ever going to start?

JERRY: It's just about time, Dear.

(*Now the lights go out, and the theme music begins.*)

VOICE: And now, "The Return of the Killer Squash." I want to warn you, ladies and gentlemen, if you have a heart condition, you may want to leave. You could be frightened to death!

(*All actors assume air of watching the movie, except* IRVING *and* BETSY, *who of course, are in their own world. At this time* SARAH LOU *arrives. She pushes her way to the empty seat between the couples. She is loaded with her treasures and can hardly fit into the seat. As she goes past* JERRY *and* RACHEL, *they move as if trying to see the movie.*)

(*Meanwhile, the sound track continues. As soon as* SARAH

LOU *gets settled, there is a horrifying scene on the screen. The actors respond with terror as they watch the imaginary scene.* JERRY *and* RACHEL *hold each other. The boys hide their faces, peeking between their fingers.* IRVING *and* BETSY *are oblivious to the movie, still gazing at each other, whispering, etc.* SARAH LOU *looks at the screen as she eats ravenously, eyes never leaving the screen and mouth never missing a bite.*)

(*Suddenly, the film breaks. We hear loud and muffled protests as the theater goes totally dark. It is important that the room be completely dark. Sounds are most important. Sounds: scuffles, feet moving, protests. As Suddenly as it went dark, the lights are back on.* DENNIS *has moved between* BETSY *and* IRVING, *holding her hand and giggling.* SARAH LOU *has not lost a beat. She is still eating.* JERRY *and* RACHEL *are trying to regain their composure: they were caught kissing. The movie resumes.*)

POLICEMAN (Offstage): The killer squash has escaped, men! He could be loose anywhere. Spread out and look everywhere! Who knows who his next victim will be?

(*Just then the* SQUASH *enters. He moves slowly down the aisle among the audience. The audience will spot him before the actors. All at once* RACHEL *spots him. She screams. She stands up and attempts to pass* SARAH LOU *and her feet become tangled.* JERRY *is right behind. They finally manage to escape and run from the theater. The boys are next, screaming at each other, "See, I told you we should have listened to Mom and Dad." Finally,* IRVING *and* BETSY *become aware of the* SQUASH. *They also scream and run out. The squash sits down by* SARAH LOU. *She offers him some popcorn and they continue to watch the movie.*)

(*Blackout*)

Undercover Agents

CHARACTERS

Man One
Man Two

COSTUMES

trench coats
hats
newspapers

SETTING

The setting is a park bench. Man One is seated at one end of the bench reading his newspaper. Man Two approaches, sits down on the other end of the bench and opens his newspaper.

Man Two (*In loud stage whisper*): The cow jumped over the moon.

Man One: The little dog laughed.

Man Two: Have you got them?

Man One: Got what?

Man Two: You know—*them.*

Man One: Oh. No, Jones has them.

Man Two: Where is Jones?

MAN ONE: I'll tell you where Jones is. You go through the department store on the corner . . .

MAN TWO: He's in the department store?

MAN ONE: No. I'm trying to tell you where Jones is. You go through the department store on the corner. Go out the back door to the alley.

MAN TWO: Go to the department store on the corner. Go out the back door to the alley.

MAN ONE: Right! Then you walk down the alley to the street.

MAN TWO: Walk down the alley to the street.

MAN ONE: Cross the street.

MAN TWO: Cross the street.

MAN ONE: Cross the street and go into the deli and ask for Sam.

MAN TWO: Go into the deli and ask for Sam. He'll tell me where Jones is.

MAN ONE: No! You didn't listen! Sam will say, "Does the cow jump high?" and you'll say, "Over the moon."

MAN TWO: Sam will say, "Does the cow jump high?" and I will say, "over the moon."

MAN ONE: Now . . .

MAN TWO: There's more?

MAN ONE: You want Jones, don't you?

MAN TWO: Yes.

MAN ONE: OK. Sam will show you a back room.

MAN TWO: Jones is in the back room.

MAN ONE: Will you listen? In the back room is a ham radio. You will call KBZX 2578.

MAN TWO: There's a ham radio in the back room of the deli. I will call KBZX 2578.

MAN ONE: Then when you get KBZX 2578 . . .

MAN TWO: He'll tell me where Jones is . . .

MAN ONE: No, KBZX 2578 will sing a song. The song he'll sing is: "Mary had a little lamb." Do you know that song?

MAN TWO: Yes, I know that song.

MAN ONE: Sing it.

MAN TWO (*Sings*): Mary had a little lamb, little lamb, little lamb; Mary had a little lamb, It's fleece was white as snow.

MAN ONE: Good! Now when he finishes, he will ask you, "Where did Mary's lamb follow her?"

MAN TWO: He'll ask me, "Where did Mary's lamb follow her?"

MAN ONE: What will you answer?

MAN TWO: He followed her to school one day.

MAN ONE: Very good!

MAN TWO: But what has this to do with Jones?

MAN ONE: Will you be patient! (*He's shouting now but looks around and lowers his voice.*)

MAN TWO: OK! OK! Good grief!

MAN ONE: Now . . .

MAN TWO: You said that before.

MAN ONE: Will you be quiet! This is important!

MAN TWO: I know it's important. Tell me how to find Jones.

MAN ONE: We're almost there. Now, ask the man at KBZX 2578 ham radio, "What color is Goldilocks's hair?"

MAN TWO: I ask the man at KBZX 2578, "What color is Goldilocks's hair?".

MAN ONE: Yes, he will say "Red." Then you will say, "No, it's gold."

MAN TWO: Then he will say "Red." I will say, "No, it's gold."

MAN ONE: Then he'll tell you where Jones is. Now repeat all your instructions so I'll know that you can find Jones and get them.

MAN TWO: I go into the department store, out the back door, into the alley, out in the street, across the street to the deli. I ask for Sam. Sam will say, "Does the cow jump high?" and I will say, "Over the moon." Sam will show me to a back room. In the back room there's a ham radio. I will call KBZX 2578. When I get KBZX 2578, he will sing, "Mary, had a little lamb." (*He sings it.*) When he finishes, he will ask, "Where did Mary's lamb follow her?" And I will say, "He followed her to school one day." Then I ask the man at KBZX 2578 ham radio, "What color is Goldilocks's hair?" He will say, "Red." Then I will say, "No, Gold." And he'll tell me where Jones is. Then I will get them.

MAN ONE: Yes, you can get them, but do you know what to do with them?

MAN TWO: Of course, I know what to do with them!

MAN ONE: What are your instructions?

MAN TWO: Well, I'm to take them home. Change my clothes. Get back in the car and drive to (*insert city name*). Give them to the man at the gate. Go in to my seats. Sit down. And watch the (*insert favorite ball team*) play ball. *What did you think I was going to do with them: Sell them to the Russians?*

A New Year's Resolution

A Monologue

My name is Betty—Mrs. Joseph Bellinger. The other night, seeing it's nearly time to make New Year's resolutions, we began to talk about what resolutions we needed to make. That is, Joe and I. I tell you I love my Joe, but it would take a great big piece of paper to put down all the habits he needs to change.

Well, anyway, he said, "OK, Betty, you start. Let's be really honest with each other. I'll tell you where you need to change, and you tell me where I need to change, if anything. That way we can make meaningful resolutions. You know, where we can't see our bad habits but other people can. How does that sound to you?"

Well, it sounded OK to me because I've been having a hard time trying to tell Joe what horrible habits he has. I didn't want to hurt his feelings or anything, so you can see I welcomed the chance—and it was so funny, I didn't have to bring it up. He did!

Joe said, "OK, Betty, you start. You name one thing I need to change, and I'll name one thing you need to change."

So I thought I'd start with a small habit and advance to the "biggies" later. I said, "Joe, you're a wonderful husband, but you leave clothes on the floor. They should either be hung up or put in the dirty clothes hamper."

And Joe said, "That's fair, I do forget to pick up my clothes sometimes. My mother always did that for me, but I'll make a special effort to pick up my clothes and either hang them up or put them in the dirty clothes hamper."

Then he began to smile and said, "Now it's my turn. Honey, you are a wonderful wife, but you always interrupt me when I'm telling a story, and it's quite irritating!"

"Yes," I said, "I sometimes do interrupt you when you're telling a story. Sometimes you don't get the details right, but, anyhow, I'll try to remember to let you tell the stories your way, regardless of how they come out."

And, of course, it was my turn again. I said, "Joe, you're a wonderful husband, but why do you carry around a toothpick after you've already picked your teeth? It's extra gross and yucky and repulsive."

I could see that hadn't set too well with Joe, but you've got to give him credit—he kept his cool. In fact, very quietly he said, "Betty, when you get something in your teeth you need a toothpick to get it out, or you get tooth decay—but I'll remember that it irritates you, so I'll throw away the toothpick as I finish with it."

And then it was Joe's turn again. He said, "Doll Face, you're a wonderful wife, but, you make noises in your sleep. If you wouldn't eat before you go to bed, you probably would sleep silently all night. Then I could also sleep silently all night, instead of listening to your groans, moans, snorts, and various other sounds . . . all night long."

By now Joe was no longer cool. And he was getting a little off base, because he couldn't hear himself and his symphony of snores he gave out with each night. If he had heard me, it must've been in his dreams because he sure never missed a log, sawing them, that is.

But I said sweetly, "Oh, Joe, I'm sorry if I've kept you awake. I'll give up eating at bedtime, so you won't be subjected to all the . . . snorts, was it? I might conflict with your concert of snores each evening."

Then Joe said, "Now Betty, you're getting very defensive! If you can't stand the truth, then we'd better just stop before you get upset."

Stop! Stop? I was just coming to the "biggies." I smiled and said, "Joe, you know I'm basically a very honest person, and you know that I don't have a temper. Do I have a temper? *No, I don't have a temper! Do I get my feelings hurt easily? No! And you're wrong if you say I do!"*

And then I said very calmly, "Joe, Lambykins, you're a wonderful husband, but (I was ready for the big one), *you stir your iced tea! And stir and stir and stir! It's an* absolute wonder *the bottom doesn't fall out of the glass!* On our first date you took me to that great restaurant, and you stirred your tea: I put it down to nervousness. Then . . . *then I took you home to meet my family . . . I prayed the tea would already be sweetened . . . but no! You asked my mother for sugar! And you stirred and stirred and stirred . . . you wondered why I got a headache that evening? I got a headache from hearing you stir your tea."*

Then Joe had the nerve to say, "Betty, if you're going to get emotional about this, we'll just have to stop. *And I don't stir my iced tea! What about you? You slurp your coffee, not sip, not drink, but slurp! S-L-U-R-P! Boy, when we go to the boss's house tonight, don't take any coffee. I'll be embarrassed!"*

By now, Joe was talking to himself, because I had gone into the next room to call my mother. (*sobbing*) "Mother," I said, "Joe is a beast, I'm coming home!"

But Mother said, "No, Betty, you can't come home. The house isn't cleaned up yet from the wedding."

About that time, Joe came in and put his arms around me and said, "Betty, forgive me, you *are* a wonderful wife. We've been married two days and four hours, and we've had our first quarrel. Let's make up in time for New Year's and the party at the boss's house."

Well, we made up, and my New Year's resolution is to look at Joe's good qualities. He has plenty, and if he's not perfect, neither am I. So my advice for the new year is to love a lot and forgive even more. Have a *Happy New Year*!

My Summer Vacation

(Use childish expressions and childlike voice.)

My name is Mary Margaret Gentry. I'm in Mrs. Thornton's third grade class. Every year we have to tell what we did on our summer vacations . . . so-o-o, I decided I'd just write about my vacation while it was going on . . . so-o-o, here it is!

Today, Jimmy and I—Jimmy is the kid at the beach, who was staying in the next cabin—so-o-o it was OK. Anyway, Jimmy and I went down to the beach to play. You won't believe what we saw. People were all over the place, lying on blankets, rubbing suntan oil on each other. . . . one little kid was throwing sand up in the air . . . so-o-o, it got all over his dad, and his dad said "words."

Anyway, Jimmy and I went down the beach and started building sand castles. Now Jimmy don't know nothin' about building sand castles; I knew that right away. So-o-o, I told Jimmy he was a terrible sand-castle builder, and he threw sand at me. So-o-o, I threw sand at Jimmy. Then . . . I threw the shovel, then I threw the bucket, and Jimmy cried . . . I could tell he was a wimp right away. So-o-o, I decided that I would just walk down the beach a little ways. Anyway, I think his mama is real mean. So-o-o, I saw little kids and big kids and little people and big people. I saw a sand crab, and it ran from me. I stuck my toes in the sand and washed in the ocean and picked up some shells and put them in my bucket. Once I saw a whale and maybe a shark. I watched some people play volleyball. They

118

wouldn't let me play, I was too little—big deal! I didn't want to play their dumb old game anyway!—So-o-o, I walked a lo-o-o-ng way. I was cold . . . it was getting dark . . . I was getting scared, and a big dog came up and rubbed against me, and he said, "Are you lost?"

And I said, "Maybe."

And the dog said, "I'll take you home."

So-o-o, I followed this great, big dog back to our cabin, and Mama was so glad to see me she didn't spank me for hitting Jimmy. And that's what I did on my summer vacation.

EVERETT ROBERTSON is the author of this selection, published originally in his book *Monologues* (Nashville: Convention Press, 1982), p. 95. © Copyright 1982 by The Sunday School Board of the Southern Baptist Convention. Used by permission.

A Musical Drama About the Family

CHARACTERS

FATHER: *Businessman*
MOTHER: *Housewife*
BUD: *Eight-year-old son*
LIBBY: *Thirteen-going-on-twenty daughter*
JAN: *Libby's thirteen-year-old friend*

All characters have a melody in which they sing their dialogues. Each time they "speak," the characters will sing lines to the designated melody.

SETTING

Living room of a typical home

PROPS

couch
TV set
family Bible on a coffee table

FATHER (*sings to the tune of "Down by the Riverside"*):
Hello, my family, I'm home from working hard,
I'm home from working hard,
I'm home from working hard.
Hello, my loved ones,
Come say you missed me, too,

And I'll tell you all the things that I've been through.

MOTHER (*sings to the tune of "Alouette." She rises as* FATHER *begins to sing.*):
Oh, my honey, I am glad to see you;
We have missed you all the live-long day.
Come and sit here so that I can soothe you,
Just relax, we'll listen to what you say.

BUD (*sings to the tune of "On Top of Old Smokey." Continues to watch TV.*):
Hello, my dear father, I welcome you home,
But can't this talk wait 'til this program's all gone?

LIBBY (*sings to the tune of "Jingle Bells." She is also sitting on couch but gets up to get* FATHER'S *attention.*)
Daddy, Daddy, listen now to me:
Bud has been a pest all day,
Wait until you see.
I can't bring my friends home,
He is so obscene.
Let's just send him off somewhere;
Life would be serene.

MOTHER: Children! Children! You are very rude.
Your poor father is in a tired mood.

(Knock at door. BUD *answers door. Enter* JAN *who is somewhat of a scatterbrain.* BUD *looks disgusted.)*

JAN (*sings to the tune of "Bicycle Built for Two"*):
Hi there, people! I am here, you see.
Please say Libby can go out with me;
We'll go to the mall and stay there.
The guys are such great "hunks" there,
But we won't roam, and we'll come home.

And if we're late we'll phone.

FATHER (*To* MOTHER):
I'm not sure, dear, Libby should go with Jan.
She's just a child and can
Get hurt, (*to* JAN) so go home, Jan.

MOTHER: You heard your father, now just say you're sorry;
Tell Jan, she can come some other day.

LIBBY: Mother, Mother! How unfair you are!
I can't go anywhere, now you have gone too far!

(JAN *leaves.*)

BUD: Oh, boy! she's done it!
She's talked back to you.
So why don't you hit her,
And give her her due.

FATHER: Bud, you must apologize,
That was quite unkind.
Let your thoughts unwind,
You've been out of line.

BUD: Oh, she's always right,
And I'm always wrong.
I can see how I might
Go learn a new song!

LIBBY: Listen to me, Listen to me!
Will you all be still?
Look at the fuss you've made,
I have had my fill!

BUD: What silly old girls!
They spout and they fuss.
If Libby doesn't stop it,
I think I will bust!

MOTHER: Bud, now stop it,

Stop it now, I say!
You're now grounded,
Grounded all the way!

FATHER (*Singing "Alouette" tune with* MOTHER)
Grounded for a week!

MOTHER: Grounded for a month!

MOTHER and FATHER:
You are grounded, grounded all the way!

LIBBY: Bud's in trouble,
Bud's in trouble,
Goody, goody, whee!
What a sight, Mom, you're right,
What a sight to see!

FATHER: You must stop all this fuss,
Be a sweet family,
Love each other tenderly,
Be nice and friendly.
Come on now, this is bad;
We make each other sad.
Forgive, forget, and make each other glad!

(BUD, LIB, MOTHER, *and* FATHER *move together, and finally all hug.*)

III.

IMPROMPTU DRAMAS WITH A NARRATOR

The Beautiful Princess

The following is a situation drama with narrator. It is done without a set but with some props and costuming. Actors are selected by the audience and are all male. Actions are performed and dialogue is repeated as the story is read.

CHARACTERS

NARRATOR
BEAUTIFUL PRINCESS
KING, the PRINCESS'S father
FOUR YOUNG MEN

Once upon a time there was a beautiful Princess. She was very beautiful, but very lonely. Her father, the King, could see how unhappy the Princess was. He asked her, "What makes you so unhappy, beautiful Princess?" (*The* KING *repeats the line*) She said, "Oh, Father, I don't have a handsome Prince to be my husband, and I'm lonely." (*The* PRINCESS *repeats the line.*)

Well, her father, the King, could not allow the beautiful Princess to be lonely and unhappy. He sent a proclamation throughout the land for suitable suitors to be found. Suitable, that is, for a princess.

A date was set for interviews. The day came for the handsome, suitable young men to be presented to the King and the Princess. There was a tall, handsome young man with blonde

127

hair. There was a short, handsome young man with black hair. Another was pleasingly plump and handsome with auburn hair. The fourth handsome bachelor was of medium height with brown hair.

The King said to the young men, "You must pass some tests to determine your suitability to marry a princess. Are you ready?" (*The* KING *repeats the line.*)

He first asked them, "Why do you wish to marry the Princess?" (*The* KING *repeats the line.*)

Number-one young man said, "I want to marry the Princess because she is so beautiful." (YOUNG MAN NUMBER ONE *repeats the line.*)

Number-two young man said, "I want to marry the Princess because she is so modest and kind." (YOUNG MAN NUMBER TWO *repeats the line.*)

Number-three young man said, "I want to marry the Princess because she has such beautiful hair." (YOUNG MAN NUMBER THREE *repeats the line.*)

Number four said, "I want to marry the Princess because she is so tall." (YOUNG MAN NUMBER FOUR *repeats the line.*)

Then the king said, "Now for your second test. You must prove you are physically able to be a prince." (*The* KING *repeats the line.*) The king told each prince-to-be to do ten situps. After that they were to run-in-place until told to stop. (Each one does these actions.)

Then the king said, "The last test will be a test of romance." (*The* KING *repeats the line.*) These were the instructions he gave them. Each was to hold the princess' hand for ten seconds and gaze soulfully into her eyes. Next, each young man was to kiss the princess' hand passionately. Next, a gentle embrace. (Each one carries out these actions.)

Then the king said, "This concludes the tests. We will now have our friends help us decide who is to be the beautiful princess' husband." (*The* KING *repeats the line.*)

(*At this time the* KING *and* PRINCESS *allow the audience to help them choose. This is done by applause as the narrator holds a hand above each young man.*)

The beautiful princess and the suitable prince-to-be were married, and they lived happily ever after. The losers slunk away to look for other lonely, beautiful princesses.

An Encounter in the Woods

This is an audience participation drama. All the characters should be men. Have the audience select them and also cast the drama as you call the names of the characters. This is as much fun as the drama itself.

The only preparation needed is to explain to the actors that they will carry out the actions as the story is read aloud. They will repeat the dialogue for their character.

CHARACTERS

NARRATOR
YOUNG GIRL
COYOTE
WOLF
BEAR
BIG DOG

PROPS

headscarf and basket of cookies for YOUNG GIRL

COSTUMES

simple costuming that will help identify characters

NARRATOR: Once upon a time a young girl was tripping merrily through the woods. She was coming from the store where she had bought a basket of groceries for her poor, sick mother.

Unknown to her, there were several pairs of eyes watching her from behind the bushes and trees. But she skipped merrily along, singing a song, unaware of danger. She stopped to look at butterflies. She stopped to look at birds. She stopped to pick wildflowers for her poor, sick mother.

Suddenly, a coyote sneaked from behind a tree. He said, "Give me something to eat, or I'll bite you with my big teeth." (*The* COYOTE *repeats the line.*)

The little girl said, "Oh, no, please don't bite me with your big teeth; I'll give you a cookie." (*The* YOUNG GIRL *repeats the line.*)

Just then a wolf ran from behind some weeds and said, "Give me something to eat, or I'll bite you with my big teeth." (*The* WOLF *repeats the line.*) "Oh, no," said the little girl, "Take this cookie, but don't bite me with your big teeth." (*The* YOUNG GIRL *repeats the line.*)

And then . . . a bear came lumbering from behind a tree, and he said, "Little girl, give me something to eat, or I'll bite you with my big teeth." (*The* BEAR *repeats the line.*)

"Oh, no!" cried the little girl, "take this cookie, but please don't bite me with your big teeth." (*The* YOUNG GIRL *repeats the line.*)

And then . . . just as the little girl began to be afraid the animals would take all the food from her poor, sick mother, a great bi-g-g-g-g dog jumped from behind a stump. He growled at the coyote. He growled at the bear. He growled at the wolf and said, "Beat it, you bums, or I'll bite *you* with my big teeth." (*The* BIG DOG *repeats the line.*)

The dog growled again and the coyote and the wolf and the bear fled into the woods, crying piteously.

The little girl patted the big dog, gave him *two* cookies, and they went off to the little girl's house to take the groceries to her poor, sick mother.

THE MORAL OF THIS STORY IS:
NICE ANIMALS GET TWO COOKIES!

The Wooing of Lovely Deer Eyes

This is an audience participation drama. This calls for a narrator (either male or female), three men, and one woman. Have the audience select them and also cast the drama as the narrator calls out the names of the characters. This is a part of the fun of the drama. Actors are to pantomime the action.

CHARACTERS

CHIEF SOARING EAGLE
BRAVE PANTHER
LOVELY DEER EYES
RUNNING COYOTE
NARRATOR

Once upon a time there was an Indian Village. In this village was a chief. His name was Soaring Eagle. There were many braves in his village, but one was braver than all the rest of the braves. His name was Brave Panther.

There were also many beautiful maidens in this Indian village. But there was one more beautiful than all the rest. Her name was Lovely Deer Eyes. And you guessed it! Lovely Deer Eyes loved Brave Panther, and Brave Panther loved Lovely Deer Eyes.

But the not-so-brave Running Coyote also loved Lovely Deer Eyes.

One day Lovely Deer Eyes was washing clothes at the edge of the stream. Brave Panther came by to talk to Lovely Deer Eyes.

Brave Panther looked deeply into Lovely Deer Eyes' eyes. Lovely Deer Eyes looked deeply into Brave Panther's eyes. Brave Panther took Lovely Deer Eyes's soapy hand and held it tightly. Lovely Deer Eyes and Brave Panther were unaware there was anyone else in the world but the two of them. But hiding in the nearby woods was Running Coyote, watching them sneakily from behind a tree. He saw Brave Panther hold Lovely Deer Eyes's hand. He saw the gaze of love on their faces. He became angry, so enraged that he rushed from behind the tree and began to wrestle Brave Panther. They fought, and Brave Panther fell and struck his head on a stone. (P-o-o-o-r Brave Panther.)

Running Coyote grabbed Lovely Deer Eyes. She screamed! She struggled with all her might, but Running Coyote dragged her away into the woods. Lovely Deer Eyes became so distraught, she fainted. (P-o-o-o-o-r Lovely Deer Eyes.)

Just then Soaring Eagle came running to the stream. He had heard the screams of Lovely Deer Eyes. He saw Brave Panther on the ground. He knelt beside him to see if Brave Panther was badly hurt. Just then Brave Panther groaned and sat up. "Where is Lovely Deer Eyes?" he shouted. "I don't know," said Soaring Eagle. They searched for Lovely Deer Eyes. They looked behind the rocks. They looked in the stream. They looked in the woods. As they were looking for her, Lovely Deer Eyes regained consciousness and ran away from Running Coyote. He chased her round and round. Brave Panther chased Running Coyote round and round. Soaring Eagle chased everyone round and round.

Suddenly they grew tired and fell exhausted to the ground, panting for breath.

After they caught their breath, Soaring Eagle made Running Coyote stand before him. He took Running Coyote's feather from his headband, broke it, and sent him away from the village forever.

Then Soaring Eagle did a marriage dance for Brave Panther

and Lovely Deer Eyes. Then and there, they became brave and squaw and lived happily ever after.

The moral of this story is: buy your squaw a washing machine and keep her home where she belongs.

IV.

RAPS

Raps

Most children and youth have a natural rhythmic instinct. Because of this, rap has become a popular music form for them. There is nothing "formal" about rapping, yet a story rap can bring home some "formal" truths in a style young people can grasp.

Some ideas for the use of raps would include storytelling, memorizing Scripture, learning books of the Bible (or the names of the disciples or the Ten Commandments, etc.), and a getting-acquainted-game. Pick a beat, and the natural rhythm of words will do the rest (with a little bit of creativity).

Following are a few examples of story raps. Using these as guides only, allow your children and youth some creative input for the production of these raps. —FRAN BAILEY

NICODEMUS
John 3:1-16

My name is Nicodemus, and I am a Pharisee (see, see)
I like to wear the finest clothes and flaunt my neat jew'lry
　　(oh yeah)
I do that so that everyone can't help but notice me
And then they'll recognize this fact: *I'm Better than thee.*
　　(He's better than you and me.)

I am a most religious man. You'll hear me speak and shout
　　(Amen!)

136

From every street corner for miles about. (b-b-b bout)
I am smart! (He's smart!) I'm very smart.
Just ask me anything, from how this *whole world* was begun
    to what makes grass so green. (What's that?)

Once (just once) I asked a question of a certain Jew.
How can a man be born again?
Impossible to do. (That's right!)
This man, named Jesus, whom I asked, said, "Listen, it's
    true."
"Unless a man is born again, he has very much to lose."
    (That's right!)

I laughed (not long) then asked again, "How can a man do
    this?" (no way)
And Jesus answered with a question I could not miss.
He said, "As a ruler of the Jews, why don't you understand?
Not of the flesh, but of the spirit must *you be born again.*"

For God so loved the world that He gave His only Son
That whosoever believeth on Him *eternal life* has *won.* (eter-
    nal life has won) (repeat)
So you be born again this day, is what you ought to pray (to
    pray),
And you'll have life without an end (an end) (no end) (it's
    true) Amen! (Amen, Amen, A-A-A Amen.)

RICH MAN, LAZARUS, ABRAHAM
Luke 16:19-31

There was a certain rich man
All dressed in finest clothes;
He lived a different life-style
From everyone we know.
(Oh yeah, yeah, he's rich! repeat)

Also, there was a poor man
Who wore some yucky sores;
He laid around the streets
For scraps of food and mores.
(Oh yeah, yeah, he's poor! repeat)
The rich man he did die,
And off to hell he went.
He never got to eat or drink
Because he didn't repent.
(Oh yeah, yeah, he's rich! repeat)
The poor man Lazarus died,
To heaven he did go;
All the pleasures he'd missed out on
Were given him twofold.
(Oh, yeah, yeah, he's poor! repeat)
So now I ask you friends
Which are you?

(FRAN BAILEY is the author of these raps.)

V.

IDEAS FOR SHARING

An Evening of Impromptu Drama

Divide the large group into small groups of five to seven each. Give each group a one-liner to build a fun drama around. Be prepared to help with suggestions the first few times you use this type of drama, especially if you are working with younger youth.

After a period of preparation in groups, each group presents the drama they have prepared.

Examples of one liners:

Claire (or John), we've got to stop meeting like this!

Well, you've got it again.

But there's no one here.

Josephine! There's four of them.

Stop crying, Daddy, we'll buy you one.

But I'm sure he was short and blonde.

How much deeper must we dig?

Guess what? No teeth!

Conductor, you went past my stop!

Once a group begins to use their imagination and creativity, there's no stopping them!

CHURCH APPRECIATION NIGHT

A youth-sponsored activity of fun for the whole church family. Object: for youth to show appreciation to the church for all the church does to nurture, provide leadership, and budget money for activities.

140

Youth departments send invitations and make posters and notices in the mailout bulletin, letting all the church family know the youth want them to attend an after-church fellowship.

Preparation: select and train several youth to lead games. Be sure the games selected are suitable for all ages and the youth know how to explain the games and carry them through.

Place chairs in groups of twenty. A good arrangement is ten chairs in a row facing another ten chairs opposite them in a row. As the people enter, seat them until each group is filled. Assign two youth to each group. The youth will lead their particular group through several games such as: "Personal Scavenger Hunt" (divide into two groups of ten and compete getting the most items as called for by the leader.)

Watch to see when games begin to die down. Declare winners and serve refreshments.

To close the fellowship, have a youth who is known by the adults to express appreciation for all the church has given them. Ask an adult (beforehand) to respond to the youth by telling them that the church loves and appreciates them.

TREASURE HUNT

Youth, adults, and children all love treasure hunts. They can be held inside or all over town. The object of a treasure hunt is to find the treasure by following a series of clues, usually done in rhyme.

To get ready:

1. Decide where to put the clues and in what order. (Ask permission before you post a clue on private property.)

2. Write the clues. Each clue should lead logically to the next clue. Have about six locations with the treasure at the last one. The treasure can be valuable, funny, or symbolic.

Example: Clue #1 Please be wise, please be smart,

Now's the time for you to start

Down Main street all the way;

Find a street that rhymes with maze.
Look for a street light, there's just one,
On which #2 clue is hung.
(The clue is on a street light on Hayes street)

3. Make enough clues for each team to take one at each location, or have each team copy the clue at the site. Be sure you do not deface any property.

4. On the day of the party, put out clues about an hour before the party is to begin.

5. If the hunt is to be in the city limits, notify the police of what you are doing and where the clues are located. They will be glad to know what people are doing running around town looking under porches and behind buildings.

6. IMPORTANT: If this is for a youth group, go in groups of four or less with an *adult* driver for each car.

To Begin: For a large group, divide into teams. Each team will have a captain, who will have the final say about the location of the next clue, although all the team will work together to solve the clues.

For a small group, divide into pairs. Now you are ready to give the groups the first clue. Allow one phone call per team back to the starting point in case they become hopelessly lost.

When all the groups are back, celebrate with refreshments and all the stories of how the clues were solved or not solved.

LIP SYNC

When Walt Disney made animated cartoon movies, lip sync became a necessary drama medium. This type of pantomime is very effective and extremely funny. A whole evening, or just one number in a variety of dramas, is unusual and refreshing.

"It looks easy. Simply play a recording and move your lips to it." Not so! To be effective, rehearse! Rehearsal in front of a mirror for timing and facial expression is absolutely necessary for good production and finished presentation. Plain and exaggerated moves are best.

Here are some suggestions:

1. Pick a recording to fit the theme of the program. Take into consideration the age of the audience. Be sure there are no suggestive lyrics. To pick a recording: (1) Listen and visualize the possibilities for movement. Fill the imagination with pictures. (2) Create ways to bring them to life. Some possibilities would be: songs of the sixties, seventies, and early eighties, collections of the Beatles, the Beach Boys, Peter, Paul, and Mary, Johnny Cash, Kenny Rogers, etc., are good sources. But the possibilities are unlimited.

2. Each person involved should perfect his or her own lyrics alone, then rehearse with the other participants for timing, accuracy, and blocking.

3. Costume creatively. Often the costume makes the pantomime work. It gives the audience a head start on laughter and makes the actor feel the part.

4. Props are important, although some are imagined: such as the use of "air guitars." This is nothing more than an imaginary guitar played by exaggerated movements with the music. Imagined or real, though not played, instruments make for a sense of actually performing the recording.

If done with attention to details and well rehearsed, lip sync will make for a hilarious evening of entertainment.